Maggie Quinn

SUSAN K. DRONEY

This is a work of fiction. Names, characters, places, and incidents are products of the author's imagination or are used fictitiously and are not to be construed as real. Any resemblance to actual events, locations, organizations, or persons, living or dead, is entirely coincidental.

World Castle Publishing, LLC
Pensacola, Florida
Copyright © Susan K. Droney 2017
Paperback ISBN: 9798891264052
eBook ISBN: 9781629898490
First Edition World Castle Publishing, LLC, December 25, 2017
http://www.worldcastlepublishing.com
Licensing Notes
Cover: Karen Fuller
Editor: Maxine Bringenberg

Table of Contents

Chapter One

Patrick Quinn, a thin, handsome, dark haired boy of fourteen, squared his shoulders as he looked over the soggy field. He was dressed in a tattered shirt and soiled trousers; his well-worn shoes wouldn't last much longer, but he didn't worry about himself. His family depended on him. His nostrils, filled with the nauseating stench of rotting potatoes, made his stomach lurch. This year he'd hoped for a crop. Anything to sustain them. Now it was gone. He felt the weight of the world come crashing down on him.

He stooped down, surveying the field, and then picked up a rotted potato. He studied it carefully for a few seconds, and then stood and holding it tightly in his hand, thrust his arm toward the sky.

"Why!" he cried as he dropped to his knees in the putrid field. Tears streamed down his cheeks.

****

A cottage with a thatched roof and walls made of stones sat almost obscured by the brown countryside, seeming to blend into the landscape. Once it had been a beautiful cottage with lush green grass surrounding it, but now it had fallen into disarray. Still, it was home to the proud Quinn family.

Catherine Quinn, the matriarch of the family, lay in her bed, gravely ill. She was a frail woman in her late forties, who looked much older. She'd been a beauty in her day, but now her once dark silky hair had turned gray. The past few years had taken a heavy toll on her, and now she was succumbing to the fever that had claimed so many of her loved ones. Her feeble hands clutched at her threadbare nightdress. She struggled to speak. Her once bright eyes were now dull and almost lifeless as she tried to focus.

The inside of the cottage was sparsely furnished, with many of its possessions sold long ago. The main room contained Catherine's large bed, which had been brought out of the room she'd once shared with her husband and placed in the main room to provide more warmth for her. The other two rooms belonged to her children. Next to the bed where Catherine laid, the family Bible and a bowl of water sat on a little table. The opposite end of the room contained a small wooden table with four chairs. On one wall was a long shelf where food and dishes were stored. All of the furniture was crudely made. A large window stood at the front of the room, and a smaller one at the opposite end. The walls were bare except for some religious pictures. The floor had no covering, and many of the boards were rotting. A large fireplace took up almost one entire side of the room, and was used for cooking as well as heat. The home used to be filled with fine furniture and two couches and comfortable chairs. They were gone now, having been sold to purchase food for the family and pay the ever increasing taxes. But it was never enough, and money was as scarce as food.

Catherine shifted in the bed. She opened her mouth and again struggled to speak. Her words were faint and garbled.

Maggie Quinn, a beauty at the age of twenty-two with flowing dark auburn hair, looked up from where she sat at the table quietly mending her brother Patrick's shirt. Around the village, Maggie Quinn was known for her determination and strong willed feisty character. It took a lot to break her spirit. Not even this desolation could break her pride in her beloved Ireland. The land would come back, she was sure of it, and voiced it to whoever would listen. Soon the fields would be prosperous, and there would be enough money to purchase proper food and clothing once again, she would say. But friends were long gone, and the family rarely had a visitor... not even Maggie's fiancé Ian O'Malley. But she knew that he had his own family and crops to deal with. His family hadn't fared any better than hers. The lazy days of strolling through the meadows were gone, but she prayed every day that they would soon return. When they did, though, she knew nothing would be the same. Those taken due to the fever would never return. A pang pierced her heart.

Maggie glanced at her mother and quickly stood up and smoothed her long skirt. She noticed a small hole in her linen blouse and made a mental note to repair it after she was done with Paddy's shirt. Her heavy shoes made clacking sounds across the floor as she made her way to her mother's bed.

"Ma, lie back and rest. Keep your strength." She dipped a cloth into the bowl of water and gently wiped her mother's feverish face.

"Maggie, where's Paddy? Are the potatoes good this year? Do we finally have a crop?" Her feeble hand touched Maggie's.

Maggie had to lean close to her mother to hear her weak raspy voice as she paused after each word, struggling for air. She knew it took almost every ounce of strength her mother possessed to speak at all. It broke her heart seeing her this way.

"He'll be home soon, Ma." Maggie set the cloth back in the bowl, hurried to the other side of the room, and retrieved a chair. She brought it over to the side of her mother's bed, and sat down and took her mother's hand in hers.

Catherine smiled at her.

"Sleep now, Ma." She began humming a tune, a favorite of her mother, and one she remembered fondly her mother singing to her when she was a child.

"I sang that to all my children." Tears came into her eyes. "Those were good times. We were happy and healthy."

"Yes, Ma, you did. It's always been my favorite." She smiled back at her mother, patted her hand, and began humming again.

Catherine listened for a few minutes and then spoke again. "What happened to the land we used to know, Maggie? Why couldn't we stop it?"

Maggie closed her eyes. She remembered the lush green fruitful fields. Her mother was right. Those had been good days. Days they never thought would end. A future they never could have foreseen or dreamed possible. Now those carefree days seemed like a lifetime ago. "I don't know, Ma. I fear only God can answer that." She picked up the Bible and began to read out loud.

Catherine settled back onto her pillow and closed her eyes, but didn't sleep.

A few minutes later the cottage door opened. Maggie closed the Bible and set it on the table. She watched her brother Patrick as he hurried over to their mother's bed. He looked tired…no, he looked defeated. His boyish face was haggard from hard work and worry. His youth had been stolen from him, and she mourned for what he had sacrificed...for the carefree days of youth he would never know. She met his sad eyes and braced herself for the news he would soon be delivering.

Patrick bent and kissed his mother's forehead. "Are you feeling better, Ma?" he asked softly.

Catherine raised a feeble hand to his cheek. "The crop. Is it good, Paddy?"

"Don't you fret. We'll be fine, Ma," he answered reassuringly.

She flashed a faint smile. "Yes. The Lord always provides. Now times will be good again." She drew a ragged breath.

"You didn't answer my question. Are you feeling better?" He looked into her feverish face.

"Now that you're here with the news, I am."

Maggie saw a spark of life come back into her mother's beautiful eyes, the spark that had been missing for so long. She fervently prayed every night for a miracle. Just when she thought her mother was slipping away, she clawed her way back. Ma wasn't ready to leave the last of her children, and Maggie couldn't bear to let her go. She'd give her own life if only her mother's could be spared.

Patrick grabbed Catherine's hand and squeezed it. "Rest now, Ma, and we'll talk later."

"Yes, Paddy." She closed her eyes.

Patrick laid a hand on his sister's shoulder. "Can I talk to you, Maggie?"

"Of course." She stood.

"She's getting worse, Maggie. There has to be something we can do," he whispered.

Maggie looked into his eyes. His once bright eyes filled with hope now looked dull, as though the life had gone out of them. Her heart broke for him. Her heart broke for all of them. "We can pray, Paddy. That's all we can do."

"And where has that gotten us?" he asked dejectedly. "It won't change anything."

She glanced at her mother, who had drifted off into a fitful sleep. Deep in her heart she knew that even if they could afford it, medicine wouldn't help her mother now. But she still wished she had the money to call in a doctor. Anything to ease the suffering. Catherine tried to hide it from her the same way Da had. But she knew. The worse part was knowing there was nothing she could do to ease it. She took her brother's arm and led him to the other side of the room, where they pulled out chairs and sat at the table facing one another.

She did have a glimmer of hope, though. If what Paddy told their mother was true, they at least wouldn't starve to death. She didn't know which was worse, dying of the fever or dying from starvation. "Is it true what you told Ma, Paddy? Do we have some potatoes? Can we afford some decent food for Ma?" she asked optimistically.

"I didn't tell Ma anything, Maggie. I can't lie to her. I told her we would be fine." Patrick was thoughtful for a minute. "I suppose I was not truthful with her because we won't be fine." He ran a hand over his chin. "We have nothing, Maggie. There's nothing left! Year after year, the crop has failed. There's no hope left. The land is in ruins." He glanced around the almost barren room. "We don't have anything left of value to sell even if we could find a buyer." He shook his head. "It's done," he said wearily. "All hope is lost."

Maggie jumped to her feet. "No, Paddy! I won't give up! There has to be a way. We need to stay strong and keep our spirits high for Ma's sake. We need to keep trying."

Patrick's eyes welled with tears as he looked at his sister.

"The earth has swallowed up the beautiful land we once knew, and left nothing but a filthy putrid black mass in its place. It will never be the same, Maggie. Can't you see?" His jaw jutted out defiantly. "You are a dreamer. Your dreams never come true. This is the real world, Maggie. Why can't you see? You need to face the truth."

Maggie refused to believe what he was saying. No, she'd hold on...she had to. Her memories couldn't be all she had left. This desolation and abject poverty couldn't be all they had to look forward to. "Paddy, don't you remember how it was? We'd go out in the fields with Da, Joseph, Daniel, Colleen, and Mary and run barefoot through the lush meadows while Ma set up a picnic. Da said we'd never be poor if we kept planting potatoes and staying true to the land. It will one day be lush and green again, Patrick. Keep the faith! Don't give up hope."

He emphatically shook his head. "No, Maggie. We don't own the land anymore. It does not belong to us. We'll never own it again!" he said angrily.

"No, Paddy." She set her jaw defiantly. "Someday I *will* own this land again. Da told us if we work hard, it can be ours again. The Quinn's have been a part of this land for generations, and always will be. It's ours. Don't lose faith, Paddy."

Paddy looked at her in surprise. "Da lost it."

"It wasn't his fault, Paddy. You know that." She pursed her lips. "It was stolen from us."

He exhaled loudly. "I know. He couldn't fight the English. Maybe he should have done what they wanted. They got the land anyway."

"You don't mean that, Paddy! He would never work for them. They only got the land because of the crop failures and the taxes they imposed on us."

"No, I don't mean it," he admitted.

"Just don't lose faith. We'll find a way."

"Faith! That's all you talk about, Maggie." He quickly rose and rushed to where she stood. He placed his hands on her shoulders and stared into her eyes. "You sound like Da. Where did faith get Da? Where is he now, Maggie? *Where*? Da worked himself to death, and for what? Then Joseph and Daniel followed him. And what about Colleen and Mary? The fever took them, too." He slowly shook his head. "The girls were just babies. Ma will soon follow them, I fear. We can't save her, Maggie. Why can't you accept what's true?" A tear slid down his cheek. "Why did God not take you and me, Maggie? Did you ever wonder? Maybe He is punishing us by leaving us here and taking those we love."

"No, I won't hear that kind of talk, Paddy. Ma needs good food. Once she gets her strength back, the fever will break. I'll fix us something to eat. We'll all feel better after we have some food in our bellies." She walked over to the wooden shelf that held their food and scanned it.

Patrick joined her and looked at the almost empty shelf. He sighed heavily. "There is no food to last more than a few days. It's over...it's time to face the truth, Maggie. Please. If the fever doesn't take us, then starvation surely will. Each new day brings more misery than the one before it."

"No! I will never give up. The Lord will provide."

Patrick dropped his hands limply to his sides. "You're stubborn like Da. Listen to what I say. Where did it get him, but an early grave? Will you not listen to reason? We can do no more. It's done."

"Don't say that, Paddy," Maggie angrily retorted. "Da loved the land. It'll be fertile again. It can't be like this forever. I will never give up hope. I will not sell my soul to the English." She searched her brother's eyes. She refused to allow him to give up. He needed to stay strong. Together they would survive. They had to stick together. "Please, Paddy," she said in a softer tone. "We can't give up. There's got to be a way. You and I need to show Ma that together we are strong. We'll work to find a way. There has to be something we can do."

Patrick's shoulders slumped. "Maggie, I'm tired and hungry. My back is breaking, and for what? Our family and friends are dead or dying right in front of our eyes. We've lost the fight. The English, and now our crop failures, have defeated us. There's nothing we can do. It's only a matter of time before we—"

"No, Patrick! We are the Quinns. We will survive!"

Chapter Two

Maggie and Patrick sat at the table eating small bowls of broth. The sun had set an hour ago, and the light from the fireplace cast a soft glow over the otherwise dark room. The candles were almost gone, and both had agreed to preserve them as much as possible.

"Remember the dresses you used to make, Maggie?"

She looked up from her bowl and smiled at him. "What made you think of that, Paddy?"

He shrugged. "I don't know. I suppose I was remembering the parties. Your dresses always had the girls talking." He sighed. "I wish we had money to buy fabric so you could have a fine dress again."

Maggie chuckled. "And what would I do with such a fine dress now, brother? Where would I go to show it off?"

He looked sheepishly at her. "You have a talent."

"Little good it will ever do me."

"But you seemed happiest when you were sewing. Your dresses were your masterpieces."

She put down her spoon. "I suppose I was happy when I was sewing. I'm not sure I would call them masterpieces, but

14

I did love closing my eyes and using my imagination."

Patrick shook his head sadly. "Now those beautiful dresses are nothing more than tattered rags."

Maggie didn't respond and they continued their meal, each consumed with their own thoughts.

A loud racking cough broke the silence. Both stopped eating and rushed to their mother's side. Maggie put her arms behind her mother's back and raised her to a sitting position. She rubbed Catherine's back until the coughing subsided.

Patrick took a cloth from the bowl of water, wrung it out, and gently wiped the sweat from his mother's forehead. He placed the back of his hand over her cheek. "She's burning up with fever worse than before." He sadly shook his head as his eyes searched Maggie's.

She saw the fear in his eyes. Her own heart lurched when she looked at her mother's face, which had turned to a bright pink. It looked as though someone had set hot embers on it. "Let me get you some broth, Ma. It'll make you feel better," Maggie said softly. She hurried to the large kettle hanging over the fireplace and ladled some broth into a bowl. The broth mostly consisted of water, and she recalled the days when the kettle was filled with fresh vegetables and herbs from the garden, and the meat from their livestock. The aroma of the stew would fill the cottage as the family eagerly awaited it to finish cooking. After supper, Da would entertain them with his fiddle, and they would fall into bed with full bellies and drift off to happy dreams. None of them would have ever believed the misfortune that would befall Ireland.

Now as Maggie looked at the bowl, she wondered how long they could subsist on nothing more than slightly flavored water. They all needed food. They needed meat and fresh vegetables. She walked to the shelf and retrieved a spoon. She brought the steaming bowl of broth back to her mother's bed.

Patrick helped position his mother while Maggie seated herself on the edge of the bed. She dipped the spoon into the bowl and then brought the spoonful of broth to her mother's lips. Catherine refused to part her lips.

"Take some broth, Ma. Please," Maggie pleaded. "You'll feel better."

"No," Catherine said faintly. "Come closer, my children."

Patrick dropped to his knees by the other side of the bed and took his mother's hands, while Maggie set the bowl on the table and then sat quietly looking at Catherine's drawn face. Every breath she took was an effort as she struggled to speak.

"We're here, Ma," Maggie whispered. "Paddy and I are here."

"Where's Paddy?" Her faded eyes struggled to focus. "Paddy?"

"I'm here, Ma." His eyes welled with tears and he swallowed hard.

Catherine slightly turned her head and focused her eyes on Patrick. Maggie leaned closer and Catherine, with great effort, slightly turned her head as her lips tried to form a smile. "My beautiful children." Her voice was growing weaker, and Patrick and Maggie had to strain to hear her. She paused and drew a ragged breath after each word, struggling to make herself heard.

Every breath she took was labored as though it would be her last, and Maggie swallowed the lump in her throat as she listened. Her eyes misted, but she knew her mother couldn't see. "Don't try to talk, Ma," Maggie said quietly. "Keep your strength."

"No. I need to talk."

Maggie glanced at Paddy. His eyes revealed that he was as frightened as she was at their mother's worsening health. She didn't know how to help her mother and did the only thing she could do, which was to offer up another silent prayer for her healing. But she had to face the truth. The Lord would soon take her beloved mother the same as He'd taken Da and her brothers and sisters. She wanted to scream and pound her fists. What had they done to deserve this? She drew a deep breath. No, her faith was being tested. She had to hold on. She had to accept whatever burdens the Lord had placed on their family. She couldn't forsake everything Ma had taught her.

"Maggie, you remind me so much of your father. You have his love for the land. You have his courage and strength of character."

"And Da's red hair and stubbornness to match," Patrick said in an attempt to lighten the mood.

Catherine laughed weakly. "My sweet Paddy. The man of the house. So much laid on your young shoulders. I'm sorry, my son."

"I have strong shoulders, Ma," Patrick replied. "Please take some broth now."

"I'm not hungry. Save it for yourselves." She sank back into the pillows and immediately began coughing again.

"Ma!" Patrick said, alarmed at the strangling sounds coming from her throat. He put his arms around her and raised her to a sitting position. The coughing slowly subsided.

Maggie looked at Patrick. His eyes were filled with sorrow, but became brighter as Maggie began rubbing her mother's back and her breathing became less labored.

"Rest now, Ma. Please?" Patrick pleaded.

"There'll be time for that later." She swallowed.

Maggie noted how difficult swallowing seemed to be.

"Have some water, Ma. You're parched. Let me get you a cup."

"No," she said in the same raspy hoarse voice. "Tell me about the crop, Paddy. Is it good? Tell me the truth. I hear you and Maggie whispering. Don't lie to me, Paddy."

Maggie's eyes pleaded with Patrick. She shook her head and Patrick nodded. She knew her mother couldn't take the bad news.

Patrick came around the bed and seated himself in the chair next to the bed. He took his mother's frail hand in his and sighed heavily. "I won't lie to you, Ma." He looked at Maggie and shook his head. "The crop is gone."

Maggie had misinterpreted his nod to mean he wouldn't tell her. If she was going to leave them, let her go with peace. She couldn't bear for whatever time her mother had left to be fraught with worry. Maggie anxiously watched her mother's face. Why had Paddy told her? Why couldn't he let her believe they would be fine? She saw the hopelessness in her mother's eyes. The will to fight to live was gone. Ma had no reason now. She could do nothing to protect her children.

"All of it? There's nothing left?"

Paddy blinked and bit his bottom lip. "Yes, Ma. We have nothing left," he replied quietly. "The fields are in ruins. As they were the year before. Now worse."

"All hope's not lost, Ma," Maggie quickly said. "The next crop will be good. We still have five potatoes I put away." She looked confidently at her brother. "We'll survive, Paddy. We need to hang on until next year."

Patrick's forehead furrowed. "No, Maggie. Even if we could find enough food to see us through, there will be no crop next year or the year after that. Don't you see?"

Maggie smiled as she looked at him. "But Paddy, we have

the potatoes I saved out."

He shook his head. "No, Maggie, the five potatoes are gone."

Maggie clutched her chest. "Gone, Paddy? No. I put them in a safe place. Da said to always save some out no matter how hungry we may be. Then we will always have a potato to plant."

He shook his head and lowered his eyes. "I found them and planted them with the others, Maggie. This year I was certain we'd have a crop with the small part of land that I thought hadn't been ruined. But the ruination spread." His forehead creased. "Even if I hadn't planted the potatoes, they still would have rotted where you'd hidden them. All of the farms of our neighbors lay in the same ruins as ours. Even if we had an abundance of potatoes to plant next year, the fields won't come back for years." His lips trembled. "The land is ruined, Maggie. Better to face it and stop your foolish dreaming."

Catherine looked at her son and sighed wearily. "Then it is done. There's nothing left to do."

Maggie refused to give up. "No, Ma. Next year will be better," she said determinedly. "The fields will be green again. The curse of our land will surely be over. It can't go on forever."

"Is this true, Paddy?" Catherine asked. "Do you think this curse on our land could be done next spring?"

"No. As I said, it could take years." He slowly shook his head back and forth. "Even if a miracle made the fields fertile again, Ma, we have no potatoes to plant. We have no money to buy any even if there were some for sale," Paddy replied. "That still won't help us through this winter, either."

No, Maggie thought. Ian would surely not let them starve.

He'd helped in the past, believing it his duty ever since he'd asked for her hand in marriage. A marriage that would have taken place if not for the bad luck that had fallen on both families. "There is hope. I can ask Ian for a potato. Surely he will spare one for us. Maybe he has some that didn't go bad. And he will see us through the winter."

Patrick rose. "Maggie, there are no potatoes to be found in the county. Those that weren't foolishly planted all went bad, too. The potatoes are *all* gone. There's nothing left!" He peered across the room for a few seconds and then brought his eyes back to Maggie. "Even if we were fortunate to find a potato, we don't know that we would prosper ever again. Can't you see what I've been saying?" he asked in frustration. "It could take years for the land to recover. How do we live till then?" He swallowed hard. "It's done. Ireland will never be the same. The Ireland we knew and loved is gone forever."

"No, Paddy! We can't give up. I won't give up. We need to keep remembering the way it was."

"Remembering won't fill our empty bellies, now will it, Maggie? Remembering won't pay the rising taxes from the English, now will it, sister?"

"Paddy, just try. Don't lose hope. We used to have plentiful vegetables from Ma's garden. It *will* be that way again. We used to have such fun dancing and singing with our friends. The laughter and happy times." She glanced at her mother. "Ma, remember the large parties every spring and fall with the music, dancing, and tables laden with food and treats? And Da. The beautiful sounds that came out of his fiddle. Ma, please remember. We danced and clapped our hands while Da got everybody's toes tapping. And you, Paddy, Da taught you to play the fiddle almost before you walked." Her eyes glistened. "I'm sorry we had to sell the fiddle, Paddy, but you'll get another one someday and we'll have good times like those again. Someday you'll play the fiddle again. We just need to hold on a bit longer," she said reassuringly.

Patrick frowned. "There's nothing left to hold onto, Maggie. Your stubbornness will be the death of you," he said angrily. "We have nothing. It's done!"

"Please, my children, don't argue," Catherine implored. "Work together."

Maggie suddenly turned. She looked in wonder at Patrick. From his expression, he'd noticed it, too. Their mother's voice was stronger and clearer. Was this the sign Maggie had been waiting for? She grinned. Things were sure to get better now. She felt it in her bones. They both looked at their mother and Maggie's heart sank. Her cheeks were even brighter red with fever.

Maggie dipped the cloth and wiped Catherine's feverish face. "Try to rest now, Ma," she said soothingly.

"You must leave Ireland for your own sakes. Go to America before it is too late." She struggled to finish the sentence and began coughing again.

Maggie set the cloth back into the bowl and gently patted her mother's back. "No, Ma. Ireland is our home. I'll never leave. Like Da, I'll find a way."

"Da's way put him in the ground," Patrick stated as he walked to the food shelf and pointed. "Look!"

Maggie joined him. She wanted to tell him he was wrong, but knew he had to relieve his heavy chest. He needed to talk even if she didn't agree. Only when he got it out of his system would he find some peace, and then together they could work on a solution to their problems.

"There is no way, Maggie! Please listen to the truth. Why are you so stubborn? We barely have enough food for a few days, a week maybe if we eat even less than we do now. What then? We've been luckier than most. You, Ma, and I are still alive. Unlike many of our friends and neighbors. Now our luck has gone, too." He turned around to face her. "Maybe Ma is right. America is a new start."

Maggie's eyes narrowed. How could she leave Ireland? America was a strange land. She'd heard wonderful stories about it, but they were only stories. How could she be certain life was better there? "Even if I agreed to go to America, we have no money for passage, Paddy. We need to find a way to stay alive here on our own land until things improve."

"Come here," Catherine called.

They walked back to her bed. "What is it, Ma?" Maggie asked dismayed that her mother's voice was weak once again.

Catherine raised a hand. "Paddy, secure passage to America for you and your sister." She slipped a ring from her thin finger and held it out to her son. "Sell this. It will fetch enough for passage."

"No, Ma! That ring is the only thing you have from your mother," Maggie exclaimed. "You've never had it off your finger for as long as I can remember."

"And what good is this ring if the last of my children starve to death? She would want it to be used for good." Her eyes clouded. "I only wish I could give it to you, Maggie, my eldest daughter, as my Ma did to me and her Ma did to her. But she will understand."

Maggie shook her head. "That ring represents the Ireland we used to know, Ma. The Ireland that will one day rise again."

"No, Maggie, that Ireland is gone forever, I fear. Take the ring, Paddy. Seek passage quickly. Don't waste time."

Patrick slowly walked to Catherine's bed. Reluctantly he

took the ring from her small hand and put it in his pocket. "I will go to town in the morning to see if I can sell the ring. The English are still buying some valuables. What they don't steal. I will book three passages."

"Two, Paddy," she insisted. "My time is near."

"No, Ma," Maggie said, alarmed. "You'll get better. I won't leave you," she cried. "And I won't leave Ian. We're to be married next spring. Have you forgotten? Ian will find a way to help us all."

Patrick's face clouded. "Those plans were made with the foolish dreams of a good crop this year," he scoffed. "And where will you live? Like the rest of us, he can't pay his taxes without a crop."

"No, Paddy. Ian is a smart man. And a hard worker. Someday we'll own a piece of land of our own and build a beautiful home for our many children. You'll see."

Patrick shook his head adamantly. "Dreamer."

"It's the dreams that keep the hope alive. It's the dreams that force me to hold on and not give up. It's the dreams that give me strength."

"No, Maggie. Your dreams are for the foolish. We're going to America. As the man of the family, that is my final word." He glanced at his mother. "I'll book the passages." He paused. "If I can sell the ring."

Maggie stepped away from her mother's bed and motioned to her brother. She led him away from their mother's range of hearing.

"Paddy, please don't sell the ring. It's all we have left," she pleaded.

Patrick pulled the ring from his pocket and held it in the palm of his hand. He studied it for a full minute. Its many jewels sparkled in the glow of the fireplace. "I know, but it will do us no good if we stay, Maggie. Ma should have sold it a long time ago." His eyes darkened. "Ireland has turned her back on us," he said bitterly.

"No, Paddy, that's not true. It wasn't always like this. You're just a boy. You don't remember the good years."

"What good years? Da lost his land to the English! It doesn't belong to us anymore. He was a stubborn man, and his stubbornness cost us our home and most of our family. We could have gone to America when many of our friends did." His eyes blazed. "I remember."

"Paddy, don't speak ill of Da. He had pride. He refused to sell out his dignity and flee to America when the others did."

"If he would have our family would all be alive today. Free in America. They wouldn't have suffered the ravages of fever and starvation. At night they would go to sleep in warm beds with full bellies." He placed a hand palm up to silence Maggie when she opened her mouth to speak. "Instead he left us to scrounge like wild animals for just a bite of food."

"That's enough! I'll hear no more," Maggie said firmly. "You should be ashamed of yourself for saying such things about Da."

Patrick frowned. "There's no use talking to a dreamer. I waste my breath." He tilted his head. "And where is your Ian? He hasn't been around in weeks. For all you know he could be dead."

Maggie sighed. "I would know," she replied, placing a hand over her heart. "I would feel it here. Someday you will know what love is, Paddy. Then you will understand." She ran a hand through her long auburn hair. "Ian hasn't come around because he's busy with his crop. The last time we spoke his Da had fallen ill and couldn't help him in the field."

"Don't you see, Maggie? He has no crop. He's no better

24

off than the rest of us. He's lost most of his family to the fever the past two years, as have we. He can do nothing for us."

"He will, Paddy. He loves me. He'll find a way."

Patrick wrinkled his nose. "Love is not enough!" he scoffed. He looked sharply at his sister. "Do you love him, Maggie? Really love him?"

The odd question threw her off guard. "What a horrible thing to say, Paddy. Of course I do. I would not agree to marry him if it were not so."

Patrick frowned. "You are a strange woman, Maggie Quinn. You act like no other woman in love."

Maggie was about to respond when a loud knock sounded on the door. She rushed over to it and flung it open. A wide smile broke across her face when she looked into the eyes of her fiancé, Ian O'Malley. He stood awkwardly clutching his hat in his large calloused hands. His clothing was torn and dirty. He was still a handsome man in his late twenties, with light red hair and bright green eyes. His eyes now had taken on a dull pallor. His once stocky body now looked thin and haggard, and his shoulders slumped as he stood looking at her.

"Ian! We were just talking about you. Now you appear. It's like magic. I haven't seen you for so long. How is your Da? How are your crops? Tell me what Paddy says is not true. Some of the farmers are certain to have good crops this year." She paused and realized she was bombarding him with one question after another while he stood looking sadly at her. "I forgot my manners. Please, come in." Ian nodded and walked inside. "Please, come sit, Ian." His pained expression startled her. "Ian, what's wrong?"

"Aye...it's gone, Maggie. Paddy speaks the truth." His eyes filled. "Da went to be with the Lord in the wee hours five days ago."

"Oh, Ian. I'm so sorry," she whispered as tears filled her eyes. She took his hand.

"My family now is all gone, Maggie. I'm the last." He reached into the pocket of his coat and pulled a paper from it. He glanced at it and then thrust it at her. "My taxes have gone up. I have no money. It's only a matter of time before I am evicted. How much can one man take?"

Maggie's heart broke for him. "Stay here with us, Ian. Paddy and you can work the land together. Next year things will be better. After we marry, when the land thrives again, we can make a home the way we planned," she said optimistically.

"No, Maggie, Ireland has turned her back on me. I am done with her," he spat out bitterly as he pulled his hand from hers.

"No, don't say that, Ian. You sound like Paddy. We can't give up! That's what the English want us to do. We have to show them we are stronger than that!" she insisted.

Ian shook his head. "We aren't strong. Our only choice is join them or flee. We will never be as before. You need to listen to your brother. There's nothing left for us here except starvation and death if we stay and try to fight for Ireland." Catherine's ragged coughing caused him to pause, and he looked toward the older woman's bed. "Is your ma any better?"

"No," Maggie said quietly. "If she has proper food, she will survive. I'm sure of it. I feel it in my bones."

"And where will you get this food?" Ian asked. "Our neighbors are killing each other for just a bite." He ran a hand through his unkempt hair. "Bodies litter the road to town. If you be so lucky to make it to town, it is overrun by scoundrels."

"But there has to be a way, Ian. I refuse to give up. How many times can I say it?"

"You're a stubborn woman, Maggie Quinn. That's one of the reasons I love you." He peered into her eyes. "I'm leaving for America. Come with me, Maggie. There's a boat leaving in a few days. My friend is in charge of one of the boats that run the passengers to Dublin to board the ship. I have secured us passage on his boat and on the ship, but there isn't much time."

"Where did you get the money, Ian?" she asked. "I thought you had none."

"It doesn't matter. I found a way." His face flushed and he avoided looking into her eyes.

"Playing cards, I suppose," she said distastefully.

He frowned. "What does it matter? It's a way out. I'm tired of being hungry, Maggie."

Patrick had been quietly listening as he stood next to his mother's bed. He pulled a covering up around her neck, then bent and kissed her forehead. He walked over to where his sister and her fiancé stood. "What will you do in America, Ian? Is there work for us?" he asked hopefully.

Ian studied him. "I've been told that the opportunities are endless. A man can make his fortune there. First, I need to convince your sister to come to America with me." He smiled at her. "We can be married there, Maggie." He turned and looked at Patrick. "With your permission, Patrick."

Patrick smiled brightly. "Of course. Go, Maggie. This is your chance. I'll come later when Ma is strong enough to travel. I promise."

She adamantly shook her head. "No, Paddy. If I have to go, I won't leave Ma and you. I gave Da my word that our living family would never be parted."

"Da would want you to go," her brother insisted. "He would never want you to stay or hold you to your word if he knew what has happened since he left us." He set his jaw firmly. "I am now the man of the family, and I tell you to go with Ian. I will join you later with Ma."

"Maggie!" Catherine's voiced called out, startling them.

Maggie was surprised at the once again renewed strength in her mother's voice. She *was* getting better! The fever would soon break. She knew God hadn't turned His back on them. Her step was lighter as she hurried to her mother's side, followed by Patrick and Ian.

"Yes, Ma? What do you need?" she asked softly.

"Go with Ian, Maggie. Take Paddy with you. I'll be gone before the next ship sails. Please, do as I say. Go to America."

Maggie's forehead wrinkled as she peered into her mother's face. "No, Ma, that's the fever talking. It's not your time. You'll soon be well again." She flashed a weak smile. "Your voice is strong, your body is next to be strong." She touched her mother's feverish cheek. "You'll soon be well again, and it won't be long 'till the earth is renewed. We'll enjoy the bounty from your garden by this time next year. It will be good again."

Ian took Maggie's arm and pulled her aside. "I only secured passage for you and me."

"I won't leave Ma and Paddy. I told you that. I will go, but only if they do, too. If they aren't on the ship, then I won't be either."

"You'll leave me to go alone then?" His eyes narrowed.

Maggie was torn. Why was he making her choose between her family and him? Had the deaths in his family turned his heart cold? Maybe they had. Was he jealous that she still had

Ma and Paddy? Couldn't he see that they would become his family, too? Now, as she looked into his eyes, she saw that they had lost the joy they used to hold. Did they even hold true love for her anymore? Of course they did, she admonished herself, or he wouldn't want her to go to America with him. But she couldn't. It wasn't fair for Ian to make her choose. "Only if I have to," she answered truthfully.

Ian's eyes narrowed. "Your ma won't survive the voyage, Maggie. I've been told it's a long, rugged journey."

"I'm sorry, Ian. I won't leave my family," she said firmly. "If you truly love me you won't ask me to."

He pulled on his chin. "Let me talk to my friend to see if there is a way. It wasn't easy to seek passage for you and me. I've already been promised work in America."

"You should have asked me first," Maggie stated. She put her hands on her hips and looked defiantly at him.

"If we were married, there would be no need," he replied sternly.

"Aye, but we're not. I have my own mind, married or not, Ian O'Malley, and you'd best not forget it. I don't want to leave Ireland, but if I must, I won't go without what's left of my family."

Ian nodded. "So be it, then. Do you have any money? Passage is expensive."

"No." She wrung her hands. "You know that, Ian."

Patrick pulled his mother's ring from his pocket. He held it up, stared at it for a few seconds, and then handed it to Ian. "Take this. It should fetch a good price to the right buyer."

"No!" Maggie cried. "Please don't sell Ma's ring, Ian. Please! We'll find another way to get the money."

Ian studied the ring. "There's no time. Maybe my friend can sell it to one of the ships' captains. If not, Maggie, you have some heavy thinking to do. There's not much time."

CHAPTER THREE

Maggie shook herself awake. She'd dozed off in the chair by her mother's bed. Patrick had gone to bed hours ago. What had awakened her? She shook the remnants of sleep off and realized what it was. Her mother's breathing was raspier and labored. She quickly took her mother's hand. "Ma, Ma!" she cried.

Catherine didn't respond as she struggled for air.

Alarmed, Maggie jumped up and stood staring down into her mother's almost lifeless face. Fear gripped her heart as she ran to the small room where Patrick slept. She shook his shoulder. "Paddy! Wake up! Hurry!"

Patrick groggily opened his eyes and sat up, rubbing the sleep from his eyes. "What is it, Maggie? Has Ian returned already?" He swung his legs over the edge of his bed.

"No. Come quickly, Paddy. It's Ma!" she said in a trembling voice.

Patrick ran with Maggie to their mother's bed. They peered down at her and grabbed her hands. Catherine smiled weakly. Her eyes seemed to be focused on something Maggie couldn't see. "Be strong, my children. Go to America." Her

31

voice was hoarse and ragged.

"Ireland will always be my home, Ma," Maggie said in a cracked voice.

Her mother looked tenderly at her. Her eyes seemed clearer now and focused. "Ireland will always live in you, my child. No one can ever take that away from you. But you need to make a new home."

Patrick cleared his throat and fought back tears. "Ma, when Maggie, you, and I get to America we'll live in a large house. We'll see the green grass again, and we'll plant a garden filled with beautiful flowers and plenty of food so we'll never be hungry again. I promise!"

Catherine smiled at him. "Yes, Paddy. You and Maggie go before it is too late."

"No, we'll all go, Ma," Maggie said with tears streaming down her cheeks. "Just hold on."

Catherine looked at Maggie and Patrick, and then closed her eyes for the last time.

"Ma!" Maggie screamed. "No, Ma!" she moaned as she fell onto the bed, weeping.

Patrick stared at his mother's lifeless body, and then laid a gentle hand on Maggie's shoulder. "She's in a better place now, Maggie. No more hunger or pain," he said in a cracked voice as he swiped at his eyes with his other hand. "If Ian can't sell the ring and secure passage for me, then you go to America with him. I'll find a way to come later. I promise. I'll find a way."

"No, Paddy," she sniffed. "You and I are all that's left of the family now. We must stay together. We *will* stay together!"

He nodded. "We will, Maggie, even if you go to America before me."

****

A few days later Maggie and Patrick sat quietly at the table. Patrick picked up his sister's hand and looked into her eyes. "He's not coming back, Maggie. It's been almost a week now. He's had plenty of time."

Her eyes widened. "No, Paddy. Ian will come. Possibly he had to travel to the next town to sell the ring."

Patrick shook his head. "The boat was to leave yesterday to go to the ship. He wouldn't have missed it."

Maggie grew fearful. "Something has happened to him. Oh, Paddy, have I forced Ian to risk his life because of me?" She bit her bottom lip.

Patrick shrugged. "Possibly he sold the ring and kept the money for himself," he replied quietly. "These are desperate times."

"He would never do that! Ian is a man of fine character. He is not a thief…especially to his fiancée," she said indignantly, looking sharply at her brother. "You should be ashamed to say such things."

Patrick sighed heavily. "Men have been known to do worse in bleak times."

"No, not Ian," she insisted.

Patrick pushed his chair back and stood. "I'll go to town and ask around if anyone's seen him."

"I'll come with you."

"No. You stay here. It's too dangerous in town when you don't have a set purpose for being there. It's not what you remember, Maggie. You'll be safer here."

Maggie got to her feet. "Promise me that you'll return, Paddy. Please promise me that you'll come back," she pleaded.

He walked around the table and put his arms around her trembling body. He kissed her cheek, and then released her. "I will. I promise."

****

The road to town was long and the path well-trodden. As Patrick walked, he remembered the happier times when he'd walked with his family. His bitterness because of their plight had pushed those memories to the back of his mind, but now he tried to focus on those long ago walks instead of the sight that now lay before him. The beautiful green fields were filled with beautiful flowers, which seemed to go on forever. The fragrance filled his nostrils with the sweet nectar. Neighbors on the road had been friendly and stopped often for a leisurely chat. Those were the good days.

Now as he trudged along the same well-beaten path, beggars came up to him pleading for whatever he could offer. His heart sank when he recognized some of them as former schoolmates. Their families had suffered the same fate as his. Some were worse off, having already been evicted from their homes.

As he rounded the bend in the road, the stench of death permeated his nostrils. Bodies were lined up along one side of the road. He turned away from the site and vomited. Tears stung his eyes at the haphazard way the bodies had been discarded, as though their lives had never mattered. But they did matter. They all mattered. Many of them had no one to mourn their passing. Was this all that was left? He cried silently. He crossed himself and offered up a prayer for their souls. He rubbed his eyes as he walked trying not to look at either side of the road. Several times he stopped to rest. In the past, this trip would have been made with little effort. Today hunger overtook him, which caused heavy fatigue to settle into his bones. Even though he was starving and fatigued, he sensed the urgency to make it to town before nightfall. The town might be dangerous, but he knew that the dark road traveled alone at night would be even worse.

Darkness descended as Patrick finally stepped foot into town. He walked slowly, amazed at the swarming crowds of people. He carefully scrutinized the crowds for any sign of Ian. A few large men with ruddy complexions and broad rugged shoulders were organizing several men, women, and children into groups. Some of the faces as they paused to look at him were filled with hope, others with fear. He walked next to one group and stopped. The man organizing the group watched him warily. The man was massive in both girth and height.

"You'll have to wait your turn," the man says gruffly. "The boats are full."

"I'm looking for someone," Patrick replied.

"Who?" the man asked as his eyes gave him a swift once over.

"Ian O'Malley. Do you know of him?"

The man shook his head. "Never heard of him. Who's he work for?"

"He has a friend who works on one of the boats," Patrick explained.

"What's the name?"

"I don't know," he replied with a shrug. "Ian was to secure passage from his friend for himself, my sister, and me."

The man stared intently at him. "Are you trying to sneak on one of these boats?"

"No...no, I'm trying to find out what's happened to my friend." Patrick knew the man didn't believe him. He was sure that many probably did try to sneak on the boats. They'd risk their lives to get away from the decadence their lives had turned into.

The man's eyes narrowed. "If I catch ya trying to sneak on

one of the boats without paid passage, I'll kill ya myself. Now get out of here!"

Patrick knew he should get out of there as fast as his legs would take him, but he couldn't. He needed answers. "When does the next ship to America sail?"

"Not for days. One left a couple of days ago. They come and go. They're all filled for weeks. Even if they weren't, I doubt from the looks of you that you could afford passage."

Patrick once again scanned the groups of people. They held tightly to their small bags, probably all they had left in the world. Maggie and he fared no better. None in the group looked any better off than he did. "Thank you," he said to the man. "I'll be on my way then."

The man's demeanor softened a little as he scrutinized Patrick. "Go home, lad. It's not safe to be hanging around here. Especially at night."

Patrick nodded and continued walking. He looked at the rundown pubs, shops, and flats. His memories took him back to the clean, cheerful, and sturdy establishments of the past. Time and circumstances had taken their toll, and his heart told him only a miracle could bring it back. As he walked by one of the pubs, loud music and boisterous voices caused him to stop. Possibly Ian had stopped in one of these pubs for a mug of beer and to play cards. He looked at the faded sign. O'Riellys. He walked slowly into the pub, and straight ahead saw a rugged well-worn wide bar.

"What will it be?" the bartender asked without looking up from where he was mopping the top of the bar with a dirty rag.

"Nothing, thank you," Patrick said, trying to steady his voice. He'd never been inside a pub before, and from the looks of this one, he didn't think it would be a place he'd enjoy inhabiting as he observed two men arguing loudly and another group exchanging blows. "I'm looking for someone. I thought he might have stopped in here."

The bartender slammed his large palms on top of the bar. "Look around, lad. Men come in and out all day into the wee hours of the dawn. I give them mugs of beer and whiskey. They tell me of their woes, but not their names. And I don't ask."

"I just thought—"

"I got work to do," the man said cutting him off. "You want something or not?"

"No...thank you."

Patrick kept his eyes focused straight ahead as he exited the pub. He didn't want to make eye contact for fear of causing the men to target him for fun. Patrick stood outside of the pub for a few minutes wondering what to do. He didn't know where to turn. Ian could be anywhere. Patrick was sorry he'd given Ian Ma's ring. Maggie and he would surely starve to death now. He didn't know what to do, but refused to believe that Ian would deceive them like this. The families had known one another for all their lives. His heart was heavy.

Suddenly the thought struck him that possibly Ian had met with an unfortunate fate. Patrick decided to check every pub in town. Maybe someone would recognize the name and remember him. He spent the next few hours asking every barkeep on the road if they'd seen him. No one had, and a few had thrown Patrick out before he could ask.

Dejectedly, with his head down, he continued down the road with no particular destination in mind. Patrick didn't know what to do next. He knew he couldn't return home... not yet. He couldn't bear facing Maggie. What could he tell her when he had no answers? When he had no hope for them.

Patrick stopped in his tracks when he heard a peal of loud laughter, followed by a drunkard stumbling out the door of a small dilapidated structure tucked away in a corner at the very end of the road. It seemed odd to see this structure set far apart from the others which all sat clustered together. It was in worse condition than the others.

He had nothing more to lose, so he made his way to the entrance. The drunken man tipped his hat to him and stumbled off into the night. Patrick looked up at a sign swaying precariously overhead. Kelley's Pub was scrawled in large green haphazardly painted letters.

CHAPTER FOUR

Patrick stood in the entrance of Kelley's Pub. Several crudely made wooden tables and chairs were crammed together filled with patrons in the cramped space. Smoke hung thick in the air, but no one seemed to care. A fiddler was playing a toe-tapping tune, but no one was dancing. The men were busy playing cards and drinking, some with scantily clad women by their sides. Flushed, Patrick tried not to look at the women. A long block of wood set on two stumps served as the bar and took up one side of the room. Patrick made his way over the filthy and uneven floor to the bar. He apprehensively studied the bartender. He was a medium sized man with bright reddish orange colored hair. He caught Patrick's eye and smiled.

Patrick was relieved for the friendly gesture after his harsh treatment from the previous bartenders he'd tried to get information from. When the bartender moved to where he leaned against the bar, Patrick said, "I'm looking for Ian O'Malley. Do you know him?"

"Never heard of him," the barkeep replied.

"Are you sure?" Patrick pleaded. "I need to find him."

"Don't know the name, lad," the man said, almost apologetically.

Patrick sighed as he looked into the kind eyes. "Then I thank you for your time."

"Feel free to ask around the room, but I never heard of 'um."

Patrick turned slightly and scanned the room for a full minute. There was nothing more to do. As he stepped away from the bar a large beefy hand clamped on his shoulder. He turned and looked at the man. Patrick hadn't seen him appear at the bar.

"I couldn't help overhear your conversation," the man said before Patrick could open his mouth. "I know him. Brian O'Shaunessey's the name. And you are?"

Patrick eyed the man. He was overweight and very unattractive, with dark gray hair and bushy eyebrows.

"Patrick Quinn. You're a friend of Ian's?" he asked relieved that he'd soon find Ian.

"Not friends, but I know him," O'Shaunessey answered. "Played cards with him several times."

"Do you know where I may find him?" Patrick eagerly asked.

The man downed his whiskey, and then wiped his mouth on the sleeve of his dirty coat. He set his glass down. "On his way to America. He said you'd be down here looking for him, Patrick Quinn. Better that I didn't have to come looking for what he owes. Is your sister with you?"

Patrick was confused. How did he know about Maggie? Maybe it was just a coincidence. Surely the man had Ian mixed up with someone else. "That can't be Ian O'Malley you speak of. He was supposed to secure passage for my sister and me. He and my sister are to be married soon."

40

"Your sister's name is Margaret, but is known by Maggie." Brian sneered at him. "He only secured passage for himself. She is in return for his passage."

"That's a lie! He had passage for them, and was securing passage for me and my now departed Ma."

"He lost his passages playing cards. I gave him his passage back in return for your sister."

Patrick stood quietly, trying to process what the man said. He must have run into Ian, or how would he know Maggie's name? But the rest of what he said was not the truth. "He wouldn't gamble the passages away."

"He did. I promised him one passage...for himself, in return for your sister. He's a poor card player. Men like him should not gamble." His forehead wrinkled. "That was the deal I made with him."

Patrick shook his head. "No. Ian would never do that. He would never dishonor my sister...the woman who is to be his wife. He never went to the ship. He would never leave without Maggie."

O'Shaunessey picked up a mug of beer and drained half of it before speaking again. "He got on the ship. I took him in my boat to the ship, and I was there to see him off."

Patrick refused to believe him. "Did he try to sell you a ring?"

"Now why would I want a ring?"

Patrick's shoulders slumped.

"Bring your sister to me and I'll try to find you some work. You might even make enough to buy some food." His eyes swept over Patrick. "Fatten you up a bit."

Patrick eyed him coldly. From the size of him, he looked like he'd had more than his fair share of food. "No. I want nothing from you. I'll find a way to secure passage to America for my sister and me."

Brian threw his head back and laughed mockingly. "Tell you what I'll do. Save me the journey to fetch your sister. Bring her to me and I promise you both passage to America." He finished off his mug of beer. "If you want to get to America you'll bring her to me."

"And if I don't?" Patrick asked defiantly.

O'Shaunessey's eyes narrowed and his tone became threatening. "You won't like the consequences. She was promised to me."

Patrick's eyebrows drew together. "She's no piece of property to be sold to the highest bidder!" he spat out.

"But is to settle a debt for a poor card player."

Patrick vehemently shook his head back and forth. "No! Ian wouldn't do that!"

"You don't know your friend as well as you think. These are tough times, lad. You'd be surprised what people will do."

"I'll find a way to get my sister and me to America without your help."

"With what?" He spread his hands wide. "I'll expect you and your sister before the week is through. I intend to collect on my deal with Ian."

"Then you deal with Ian O'Malley! I won't bring my sister to you," Patrick said adamantly.

O'Shaunessey clamped his heavy hands on Patrick's thin shoulders. "If you don't bring her to me, I'll personally break every bone in your body and still take her."

Patrick didn't utter another word. He knew Brian O'Shaunessey meant every word he said.

"Now go! And don't come back without her."

His words rang in Patrick's ears as he made his way out of the pub. He scanned the road from where he had come. A stiff wind had picked up so he pulled his threadbare coat tighter around himself, but it did little to stave off the dampness of the night. He noticed several groups of people who he'd seen earlier and assumed they were inhabitants of the town, but now realized their plight was the same as his. They were huddled together over barrels someone had lit in an effort to ward off some of the cold night air.

Patrick knew he had to spend the night in town. It was too late to take the long road home. He shuddered, thinking of that road in the pitch-black darkness. He began searching for a reasonably safe place to bed down. Even if a thief accosted him, he had nothing worth stealing except for the clothes on his back. Someone might be desperate enough to take his coat. Yes, these were desperate times, and he'd never realized how desperate things had become before this journey.

His bones ached more with every step he took, and sharp pangs of hunger ripped through his stomach. He glanced down every alleyway he passed. As his body further weakened and he couldn't go on much longer, he spotted an empty boarded up door down an alley. No one had claimed the spot, so he forced his weary legs to trudge forward, willing his body to reach the destination. Relieved, he sat and settled against the cold hard door. Almost immediately, he was asleep.

The following morning he awoke stiff and sore. He stood, trying to get his legs working again. He watched others who had also settled in the alley for a few minutes as they began to stir from their slumber, while some began rummaging through the piles of scraps the shopkeepers had discarded through the back doors. His stomach immediately rumbled, and he had decided to join them when he noticed they had company. Rats! His stomach lurched. What had civilization as he'd known it come to? Was this their future…was there nothing more? If this was his destiny, then he wished the fever had taken him, too.

Patrick quickly exited the alley, and as he made his way down the road, he knew he had to find work. As the man of the family, it was his duty to protect his sister. He had to keep them together. He'd find work. Patrick would do anything to put food in Maggie and his bellies, and save the rest for their passages. Maybe they could stay in their home. That was if the English didn't raise their taxes as they had for the past two years. They paid taxes on land they no longer owned, but there was nothing they could do about it.

He spent the next two days scouring the town, but there was no work to be found. He'd eaten from trash bins in front of the shops to stave off starvation, telling himself that at least most of them weren't as heavily infested with rats as the ones behind the shops. Exhausted from his futile search for work, he fell to his knees in an alley.

"What have we done to deserve this fate, Lord?" he prayed. "How will we survive? Show me the way, because I am tired and beaten down." Tears streamed down his face. Others looked at him, but said nothing. After he'd prayed for several minutes, he wearily pulled himself to his feet. He didn't feel restored. His spirit was depleted. The Lord had let them down.

He walked back out of the alley. A shopkeeper opened his door and tossed out some spoils, and he scurried to where the cakes had landed. He grabbed two before the small pile was descended upon.

Patrick dreaded the trip back home in the dark alone, but he couldn't stay another night. There was nothing for him here, and he'd rather sleep in his bed instead of in the alleyway. As he began the journey home, he didn't know how he'd break the news to Maggie. Her faith would finally be broken, as his had been. He wondered if their spirits could ever be restored. He shook his fist in anger at the sky. "Why didn't you take us too, Lord!"

Chapter Five

Maggie paced back and forth across the cottage. Where was Paddy? She anxiously wondered. It had been over two days now since he'd gone. Had he found Ian? Had he secured their passage? She wrung her hands as she peered out of the window. Darkness was once again falling. Fear gripped her heart, almost paralyzing her, and she moved away from the window. She refused to allow her imagination to run away with her when it insisted that something horrible had happened to her beloved brother.

She walked to the fireplace and held her hands out, rubbing them together. Soon there would be nothing left to burn. If they didn't starve to death, then surely they would freeze. The winter would be brutal, and with no heat or food, how could they survive? She didn't want to leave Ireland. Ian had been her last hope. Her eyes misted and her heart cried for the Ireland she once knew and the Ireland she'd always love. She looked at the paper lying on the table, which had been delivered this morning. All was gone now. The land had long ago been taken from them, but now even the house Da had built with his own two hands was gone.

She glanced at the bed where her mother had lain. Now it was cold and empty. She missed her terribly. Ma was right... she had to leave. But someday she vowed to return. Her heart would always belong to Ireland.

Maggie was startled when the door slowly started to open, and she turned from the fireplace. She was all alone and would be an easy target for someone who wanted to do her harm. Maggie quickly grabbed the fire poker and gripped it. She backed toward the shadows in a corner of the room. Hopefully she wouldn't be detected and could strike if the need arose. As the door opened, her heart leapt into her throat.

"Maggie?" Patrick called.

Maggie threw the poker aside, and with tears streaming down her cheeks ran to the door. She threw her arms around her brother. "Paddy, I was so frightened. You've been gone so long. I was making the decision to go to town in the morning since you hadn't returned."

Paddy held her close. "Wipe your tears," he said softly. "I told you I'd return. I'm pleased you didn't go to town. You should never go alone." He sighed tiredly. "It's not the way you remember." He let go of her and pulled the cake he'd saved for her from his coat pocket. "Here. I brought this for you." She started to protest, but he held up his hand. "No, there were two. I ate one. This is for you."

"Thank you." Maggie hungrily bit into the sweet cake. Her stomach was empty, but this would sustain her. At least for a little while. She'd tell Paddy the news about the house after Paddy gave her his news about Ian.

Patrick took her arm and led her to the table. He removed his coat. "It's getting cold out, Maggie."

"It's too soon, Paddy. Even the weather deceives us," she answered. "What about Ian? Have you found him?"

47

Patrick looked intently at her for a few seconds, but kept silent.

"Paddy, what is it? What's happened?"

He exhaled loudly. "He's not the man we thought he was, Maggie."

A tremor rippled through Maggie. "What's happened to him? Did you speak with him?"

Patrick shook his head. He rubbed his jaw and met her eyes. "I couldn't."

"Why not?"

"There's no easy way to say this, Maggie. I pray there was an easy way."

Maggie clutched her chest. The news wasn't good. How much more could she take? She steeled herself. "Say what you will, Paddy." She watched his pain filled eyes.

"He's on his way to America."

"Alone?" She was confused, but relief flooded through her. He wasn't dead. "Did he secure our passage?"

"No."

She gripped the edge of the table. "How do you know? Tell me everything, Paddy."

His body slumped in his chair. "It's done. It does no good to talk about it."

She sensed he was trying to protect her feelings, but she had to know the truth. "No, Paddy. It is not done until you tell me. Did Ian sell Ma's ring?"

"I don't know," he replied quietly. "I found his so-called friend. The man didn't want the ring, so he says."

Maggie's eyes widened. "His friend is lying then. Ian would have never sailed without coming back to tell us if he couldn't sell the ring."

"Maggie, listen to me. He never did secure passage for

48

you…only for himself."

"No, I refuse to believe that! He wanted me to go with him. You heard him, Paddy. He went to try to seek passage for you and Ma, too. He doesn't know that Ma has since gone to be with the Lord. Please, Paddy, tell me this is not so."

"Listen to me, Maggie," he said firmly. "Please! He promised you to his friend in exchange for his gambling losses and for his own passage to America. He deceived us. He stood here in our home and lied to all of us."

"No! I won't hear it!" Maggie stated adamantly. "He loved me. He could never do such a thing."

Patrick looked sympathetically at her. "I don't deny that he once loved you. But these are desperate times, Maggie, and he put his own needs above yours. Better to find out now what a poor husband he would have been."

Maggie didn't want her brother's sympathy. She struggled to fight the many conflicting emotions coursing through her. She didn't want to believe that Ian would push her aside to save himself. He'd been such a kind, gentle, loving man. They would have already been married if it weren't for the bad times that had befallen Ireland and their families.

Through the years both families had struggled, but Ian and Maggie had vowed that they would become husband and wife next spring no matter the circumstances. Now that dream was shattered, too, if what Paddy said was true. Had Ian sold his soul to the devil? Hot heavy tears began pouring out of her eyes. She couldn't control them as they spilled down her cheeks. Her heart was crushed.

Patrick balled his hands into tight fists and then stood up and began pacing. "If I ever see Ian again, I swear I'll murder him."

"Paddy, don't talk like that," Maggie cried.

49

He stopped and looked at her. "For once I'm pleased you refused to listen to me when I insisted you go with him. If you hadn't—" He stopped speaking when his eyes settled on the notice lying on the table. He picked it up and slowly read it. "What's this!" he demanded, thrusting the paper toward Maggie.

"I was going to tell you, but it slipped my mind with the excitement of your return," she said, finally bringing her tears under control. She sniffed and then took a cloth and dabbed at her eyes. "It was delivered this morning. We have to leave, Paddy. We have no choice now. We've now lost everything." Her lips trembled. "My heart is heavy."

Patrick set the paper back down and ran a hand through his hair. "I've let you down, Maggie. I've let our family down. Why was I so foolish to give Ian the ring? Now we have nothing of value and no hope. We'll be like those on the road to town, dying before they even reach town. Beggars they've turned into, starving to death with no one to claim their bodies. Is this what's to become of us?" He buried his face in his hands.

"It's done, Paddy. We must stay strong." She finished drying her eyes and then straightened her shoulders. "You did your best. You've kept us going for the past two years." She walked over to him and put an arm around his shoulder. "Da would be proud of you." She took his hands from his face and looked at him. "Take me to this friend of Ian's. Let me speak with him."

"Never!"

"It's our only hope of getting to America."

"Not at that price, Maggie."

"At what price then, Paddy? Listen to reason. We can't pay our taxes. I never thought I'd see this day come, but it has. We'll be thrown out of our home. We need to leave with what pride we have left." Her eyes brimmed with fresh tears. "There is nothing else we can do. Help me pack our things and you get a good rest, and then we'll be on our way at the first light."

"Maggie, the road to town is not a pleasant sight. The stench of death is everywhere."

"If I can survive the dying our home has seen, I can endure anything."

Chapter Six

Patrick held tight to Maggie's arm as they made their way down the congested road to Kelley's Pub. "Paddy, I never dreamed conditions were this bad for our people. All these poor souls begging for food and dying before our eyes. How did it come to this?"

He stopped walking and adjusted their bundle of possessions, which contained only a few changes of clothes and the family Bible, where Ma had kept all important papers. He looked at her, but didn't answer her question. His jaw tightened. "There has to be another way, Maggie. I can't let you do this. I'd rather give my own life if it would save your dignity."

"And now where would I be without my brother? We have no food or a roof over our heads, Paddy. Would you rather we starve to death in the streets like so many have? We need to be strong together. We need to carry on the family name for Ma, Da, and our brothers and sisters."

His forehead wrinkled. "If only I could find some honest work until we saved enough."

"The only jobs left, I fear, are for dishonest men."

He nodded and they resumed walking. He gripped her arm tighter.

Groups of men huddled together outside of the pubs made catcalls at Maggie, and some yelled out suggestive comments, causing her cheeks to flame and Patrick to hold her even closer.

Patrick stopped when they neared Kelley's Pub. "There he is," he whispered.

Maggie studied the unattractive man who was leaning against the wall next to the entrance of the pub. He caught Maggie's eye and smacked his lips. The sight of him sickened her. He motioned for them to come closer.

"Ian is a man of his word. Just as he described," Brian O'Shaunessey said as he leered at Maggie.

"Can you find us work? We'll earn our passage through our work. We'll pay off O'Malley's gambling debt to you."

The man laughed. "Look around you, lad. Does it look like there're any jobs to be had? Nothing's changed since we last spoke." His beady eyes swept approvingly over Maggie. "You'll earn your passage according to my agreement with O'Malley. I'm a man of my word."

Maggie doubted that. She hoped he saw the disgust in her eyes for what he was about to do. If he had a conscience he would, but she assumed he'd lost that a long time ago if he'd even been born with one.

He moved closer to where they stood and looked at Patrick. "Why don't you run along?" It wasn't a question, but more of an order. "Your sister and I are going to get acquainted."

"I am willing to do any type of work," Patrick insisted.

"Clean your ears. I told you there is none." He took Maggie's arm.

Maggie's stomach lurched as his rancid breath assaulted her nostrils. His body didn't smell much better. Patrick was still holding tight to her other arm.

"Where are you taking her?" Patrick demanded.

"She'll be back later with passage for you both." He took some coins from a pocket of the heavy dark blue woolen jacket he wore. He thrust them at Patrick. "Go get yourself a decent meal while you wait."

Patrick ignored the coins in O'Shaunessey's pudgy hand.

"Take the coins," Maggie urged.

Patrick reluctantly took the coins and clutched them in the palm of his hand. "How can we be certain that you truly do have passage for the both of us? Why should I trust you to honor your word?"

Brian yanked two tickets from his pocket. "I have them right here. The ship leaves in a few days. I'll take you on my boat to the ship, and personally escort you to the docks as I did Ian. I'll see you both safely on the ship." His eyes narrowed.

"How do I know you'll give the tickets to us? Let me hold them," Patrick said, eying the large man uneasily.

O'Shaunessey snarled. "You can have yours. She'll get hers later if she proves worth the price." He winked. "Don't worry, lad. From the looks of her, she'll be well worth the price." He clamped his beefy hand on Maggie's upper arm.

"I'll thank you to let go of my arm," Maggie said angrily.

O'Shaunessey lifted his bushy eyebrows. "A scrapper. Those are the best kind." He grinned at Patrick. "If you know what I mean. But then, you're just a lad, and have probably never experienced the charms of a feisty lassie, or any for that matter." He threw his head back and laughed heartily.

"No! I can't go through with this. I won't allow my sister to go with you. The deal is off. Come, Maggie. We'll find a way."

The man's eyes darkened. "My deal was made with Ian." He dropped Maggie's arm and thrust a raised fist in front of Patrick's face.

"I must do this, Paddy." Maggie knew Patrick wouldn't stand a chance in a fistfight with this brute. Brian O'Shaunessey would leave her brother a crumpled, bloody mess. "It's the only way. I'll return. I promise." She hugged him tightly and kissed his cheek. "Be safe," she whispered in his ear. "Pray for me."

O'Shaunessey took Maggie's arm again, pulled her away from her brother, then pulled a ticket from his pocket and handed it to Patrick.

Patrick glanced at the ticket and then stuffed it into his pocket. "When will you return with her?"

"When I've had my fill."

"I'll be back, Paddy. I promise," Maggie said.

****

Patrick watched as Brian O'Shaunessey held Maggie's arm tightly and walked several steps, and then abruptly turned a corner. He hurried to the corner and peered down the narrow alleyway. O'Shaunessey was dragging Maggie into a building halfway down the alley. Patrick's shoulders slumped. Maggie couldn't disguise her fear from him, even though her voice pretended to be calm. He saw in her eyes the fear she felt. That was something she could never mask. He'd let her down. He'd let his family down. They were all that was left now. He stood staring down the littered alleyway for a few minutes, trying to formulate a plan. He couldn't let her go through with it. But how could he rescue her? He was no match for O'Shaunessey. The man could break him in two with little effort. Dejectedly he walked back to Kelley's Pub and stood outside for a few minutes before entering.

Inside the pub he was surprised to see an empty table, and quickly walked over to it and pulled out a chair. After he was seated, he set the bundle next to his chair and looked around the nearly full room filled with loud music and boisterous men who were drinking and gambling at the surrounding tables. Smoke hung heavy in the air, stinging his nostrils. He was out of place here and he knew it. Uneasily, he continued to look around the room. He didn't know what he was looking for. Maybe a friendly face who would offer him some help. He doubted he would find it here.

Tidbits of conversations floated past him. The card playing men at the table next to his were having a heated discussion. When he heard O'Shaunessey's name mentioned he strained his ears to listen to what they were saying.

"Where's O'Shaunessey? I need to win back some of my money," an overweight burly card player asked.

The man sitting across from him laughed gruffly. "Probably with a new girl. Can't let America and England have them all," he said with a wink. "If you know what I mean." He laughed again.

Patrick studied the man. He wasn't as large as the other one, but he had a weathered face and hands like claws from the way he was gripping his cards. His teeth were half rotted, and those that weren't were yellowed. The other men joined in his laughter and began making obscene gestures as they hoisted their mugs of beer.

Patrick knew what they were referring to, and it made him sick to his stomach. He didn't want to think about what O'Shaunessey was doing to his sister right now. Tears stung his eyes. He couldn't protect her...not by himself. He drew a shaky breath. Her fate would be even worse, because he knew Maggie wouldn't willingly give in to him. She would fight even if it meant the end of her life. Tears stung his eyes. He placed his elbows on the table and buried his head in his hands. He didn't notice the chair opposite his being pulled out.

"Mind if I sit? Connor Murphy's the name."

Patrick looked up and into the friendly eyes of a scrawny brown haired boy who looked to be not much older than him. He quickly stood and grabbed Connor's extended hand, pumping it vigorously up and down. He welcomed the company. "Please sit." He quickly brushed the spilled tears from his cheeks, hoping Connor hadn't noticed. If he had, he kept quiet. They both sat.

"Are you waiting for transport to the ships in the morning?"

Patrick nodded. "Aye."

Connor glanced swiftly around the room. "Most of these are the men who will take us in the boats to Dublin."

"I'm waiting for my sister to return with her passage," Patrick explained.

Connor frowned. "I heard talk that all ships are full. Even if you could find a spot, the cost has gone up. The next boats will even be higher," he stated.

"I have my passage," Patrick said. "My sister is seeking hers as we speak. There will be room for us."

Connor frowned again. "Where is your sister securing passage?"

Patrick didn't want to answer, but it was an honest question. He briefly lowered his eyes, and then raised them again and met Connor's eyes. "These times have forced us to go against what we know is morally right."

He nodded. "Aye. My two sisters have been forced to do

the same. They were supposed to sail to America with me. We are all that is left of our family. The fever took the rest," he said in a shaky voice. His eyes misted.

"My family has suffered the same fate," Patrick said sadly. "Maggie and I are all that's left of ours." He paused as he realized what Connor had said about his sisters *were* going to sail to America. He couldn't imagine anyone not wanting to escape the fate that beheld them if they stayed. "Your sisters changed their minds about going to America? They'd rather stay in Ireland and starve to death or die of the fever? It makes no sense."

Connor sadly shook his head. He clasped his hands tightly together. "No, they were happy to flee Ireland. We were assured passage. When I came here two days ago, I was given mine. My sisters were taken somewhere else to secure theirs. I was told to wait for them at Riley's Pub down the road. They were to return later with their passages," he replied in a faltering voice. "I haven't seen them since. I've searched the town since, but no one has seen them. Time is running out. We are supposed to be on the boat first thing in the morning to go to the ship."

Patrick's heart went out to him. At least he knew where Maggie was. If he didn't he didn't know how he would cope, and wondered how Connor was able to hold it together. "Who is the man who secured your passage for you?" Patrick asked.

Connor's eyebrows drew together. "A man I met a week ago when I came to town seeking work to afford passage for my sisters and me. He asked if I had anyone else from my family seeking passage other than myself. When I told him about my sisters, he told me to bring them to town and we would have our passage. I was grateful for his generosity. He explained that it was his duty to help his fellow Irishmen."

"Do you know his name?" Patrick asked.

Connor exhaled loudly. "O'Shaunessey, he said."

One of the card players who'd earlier mentioned O'Shaunessey's name now turned in his chair and faced Patrick and Connor. "Couldn't help but overhear. Are you speaking of Brian O'Shaunessey?"

"Yes," Connor replied as a glimmer of hope appeared in his eyes. "That's the name. Can you tell me where I can find him? I'm looking for my sisters. They were last with him."

The man sitting next to the man who'd questioned them now spoke up. "He'll be around. Hard to say when," he said, eying Patrick and Connor carefully.

"He promised passage to America to my sisters and me."

"Did he give you passage?" the man asked Connor.

"He did."

"And you?" he nodded toward Patrick.

"Aye."

"He gave you passage as promised. Get on the boat, then the ship, and leave Ireland behind, lads."

"Not without my sisters," Connor said heatedly.

"My sister is with him as we speak," Patrick said quickly.

The man tilted his head toward the other men, who'd stopped playing cards to listen to the exchange. "The young lads are trying to act like men, but ignorant of the world."

The men laughed and jeered at Patrick and Connor, and clinked their mugs together.

"Your sisters will be taken care of. No need to worry. They will be fed, clothed, and have a warm bed to sleep in."

"But not often alone," one of the men added to what his friend had said, which caused another bout of laughter and jeering.

"It makes no sense what you say," Patrick said. "What's

he done with my friend's sisters and mine?"

The man lifted a bushy eyebrow. "You made a deal with him. He held his bargain. Both of you got passage."

"No! Passage is for all of us," Patrick retorted angrily. He stared into the man's cold eyes. "He gave his word to me and my sister."

Patrick's last comment caused another outburst of laughter from the men.

"As is the same for my sisters and me," Connor stated. "A man's word is his bond."

The man held his mug in a beefy hand and took a long swallow, then slammed his mug on the table and leaned forward. "Maybe you have no deal. What proof do you have that he made any such deal?" His beady eyes stared coldly at them.

A shiver ran down Patrick's spine. "A man's word is his honor."

"Your word against his. And who would believe the likes of you two ragamuffins?" he snarled. "Run along now. May your luck be better in America."

Patrick jumped to his feet, knocking his chair over. His eyes blazed. He balled his hands into tight fists. "Not without my sister! I will not leave her behind. If you know what he's done to our sisters, tell us!"

"Or what?" The man shoved back his chair and stood directly in front of Patrick.

Patrick was intimidated by the man's height and weight, but hid his fear. His adrenalin surged through his veins. "Do you know where they are?"

"Run along, or when I get done with the both of you, you won't have passage either."

Connor laid a heavy hand on Patrick's arm. "We can't

take them," he said as the other men at the table stood next to the first man.

Patrick nodded, picked up the bundle, and they walked out of Kelley's Pub amid loud laughter.

Chapter Seven

Brian O'Shaunessey roughly shoved Maggie inside a small dark room. An unmade bed dominated the bulk of the room. The room smelled and appeared to not have been cleaned in a long time. An old covering was nailed across the window, keeping the sunlight out. It was hot and stuffy. Maggie looked at the cluttered floor, which was littered with dirty clothes and empty whiskey bottles.

"Remove your cloak," O'Shaunessey ordered. "Let me get a look at you."

Maggie took her time removing her cloak. After she had, he held out a hand. She gave it to him.

He tossed the cloak on the bed and then turned his attention to her. He rubbed his hands together as he leered at her. "You're a pretty one. Once we put some meat on your bones, clean you up, and dress you in fine clothes, you'll fetch a good price."

"I'm sure I don't know what you mean," Maggie innocently said. She needed to stall him. Maggie very well knew what he was talking about, and if she didn't find a way out of this, she would never see Paddy again. She'd be subjected to a fate worse than death. Looking at him made her stomach lurch. Maggie wished she could plug her nose from the body odor that permeated the room.

O'Shaunessey smacked his lips together. "Men will pay top price to spend time with you."

"I would never do that!" she retorted. "I will only do this one time with you because you give me no choice. I need my passage to America."

His forehead wrinkled. "There are always choices. Ian O'Malley made yours." He moved closer to her. "Now you will do as I say."

Maggie eyed him coldly. "You would take me unwillingly?"

He threw his head back and laughed. "It matters little to me."

"I was a fool for believing Ian O'Malley. Did he also give you my mother's ring? Is that why you gave passage to my brother? It should have fetched enough for my passage also, and then some."

"What would I want with that bauble?" he scoffed. "O'Malley tried to give it to me in exchange for you."

Ian wouldn't do that to her. He'd never want this fate to befall her. He came from a fine family, as did she. She'd known him her entire life. They'd attended church together every Sunday before the bad times came. He would never sell his soul to the devil. "Then he didn't intend for me to be a tradeoff. He knew nothing of your intentions."

Brian scratched a jaw. "He knew, and even partook of some of the fine lassies at the pub."

Maggie felt like someone had reached into her chest and was squeezing the life out of her heart. "That can't be true."

"Think what you will. He did intend to use you. He

needed to pay off his gambling debts. At our first meeting he offered you. When he returned, he tried to offer me a ring in exchange for you."

"But he didn't want to give me to you or he wouldn't have offered the ring." She placed her hands on her hips and stared at him. "He is an honorable man."

He chuckled. "There is no honor in him. You've been deceived. When faced with no passage for himself, he gave me directions to your cottage if your brother didn't show up looking for him. He was sure you would send your brother to find him." He grinned. "He knows you well. Better than you know him."

She frowned. She still didn't want to believe Ian would deceive her, and tried to find some sense in what this vile man was saying. "Yes. He knew I would send Patrick. Ian and I were to be married. Did he also tell you that?"

He nodded. "That he did."

Her eyes narrowed. "And you never intended to give me passage. Only Patrick. How do I know for sure that you didn't harm Ian? Maybe what you say is all lies."

"Enough talk! Now you will do as I say," he said.

His face contorted into a face so ugly the likes of which Maggie had never before seen. It was a face of pure evil. She was terrified, but she had to keep her emotions in check. Letting him see her fear would be the end of her. She summoned up what little courage she could muster and told herself that fear was a sign of weakness. She needed to stay strong. She cleared her throat. "What is to become of me after you've had your way with me?"

"I said no more talk." He walked to where she stood and began to embrace her.

She placed her hands on his chest and firmly pushed at

him. She couldn't go through with it. He'd have to kill her, because there was no way she would allow this horrible man to touch her body. "No. I won't do it! I can't," she cried. "There has to be another way I can gain my passage to America."

An ugly grin spread across his face. "Your passage was never to America. The choice is not yours to make. Ian O'Malley made that choice for you. Now do as I say!"

"How could you take me against my will? Do you have no conscience?"

He sneered at her. "Your will matters nothing to me."

"You are an evil man!"

He laughed. "I've been called worse. No more talk now. I am not a patient man."

Maggie stepped back as he once again tried to embrace her. The odor from his breath and body was unbearable, and she tried not to breathe through her nostrils. She was no match for him. That was obvious. She had to keep her wits. There had to be a way to outsmart him. It would do no good to run for the door. He'd locked it behind them and put the key in his pocket. No matter what happened, she knew she wouldn't give in without a fight.

He stood looking at her. "It's your first time, I suppose." He lifted his eyebrows. "My lucky day."

Maggie kept silent as she watched his every move. She couldn't imagine that mouth near her own. His teeth were yellowed and several were missing. She bit her bottom lip to keep from crying, and prayed that he couldn't see her fear. She knew there was no hope. Images of her family floated through her mind. What would become of Paddy? He was just a boy. She had to survive. For Paddy. Maggie gritted her teeth and kept her eyes on the man.

"Maybe this will calm you." O'Shaunessey pulled a large

bottle from a pocket of his heavy woolen coat. He opened the bottle, took a swallow, and wiped his mouth on the sleeve of his coat. "Have a drink. It'll calm you." He thrust the bottle at her.

She reluctantly took the bottle, and under his watchful eye brought it to her lips. He seemed satisfied and walked to the bed, where he removed his jacket and tossed it into a corner. Maggie was relieved that he'd taken his eyes off her, because she couldn't bring herself to drink from something that had his foul mouth on it. The thought of it caused her to gag. She watched O'Shaunessey as he sat on the edge of the bed and began to remove his heavy boots. She had to think fast…time was running out. But what could she do?

Maggie glanced around the room again looking for anything to use as a weapon. Looking down at the bottle she still held in her hands, she made her decision, then glanced at Brian and drew a deep breath. This was her only chance. She held the bottle with one hand, swiftly raised her arm, and then quickly brought it down. The bottle splintered on the litter strewn floor.

O'Shaunessey instantly was on his feet. "You'll be sorry you did that!" he bellowed as he lunged toward her.

Maggie quickly bent down and picked up a long jagged shard from the bottle before he reached her. She held it threateningly in front of herself. As he came closer, she dodged out of his way.

Brian's eyes looked at the spilled liquid and then up to her hand holding the piece of broken glass. His eyes flared as he stared at her. "What do you think you're going to do with that?" he snarled.

Maggie waved the shard of glass back and forth. His eyes followed the glass. If she wasn't so frightened it might have been funny, but she needed to stay in control. It was her only hope. "Stay back, or I swear I'll cut you to shreds." Her insides were crumbling, but she couldn't let Brian O'Shaunessey see her fear. But could she shove the piece of glass through his flesh? She'd never harmed another living soul, but these were desperate times. It was survival. And she needed to survive not only for herself, but also for Paddy. She kept her eyes even with his.

"You don't have it in you." He laughed. "Now put it down, take off your garments, and climb onto the bed."

His evil laugh chilled Maggie, but she was determined to stand her ground. She had no other choice. If she didn't act now, he would surely make her pay in the worst possible way for what she'd done. It would be far worse than what he already had in store for her. "Do you want to find out what I'm capable of doing?" As she continued to stare into his evil eyes, fear suddenly left her and her body was rejuvenated with anger, anger so red and fiery that it brought out emotions she never realized she possessed. Anger for what had happened to their land, and anger towards those who had contributed to her loved ones deaths, and the plight she now found herself and Paddy in. It was men like Brian O'Shaunessey, who turned their backs on their own heritage, who made her blood run cold. They had no morals or integrity. As her anger intensified, she felt empowered with new strength. She was in control. O'Shaunessey believed she'd put the piece of glass down and take his punishment.

"This is your last chance," O'Shaunessey warned.

"Give me my passage and I won't tell the authorities what you tried to do to me." She jerked the piece of glass back and forth as she spoke.

His eyes narrowed into slits and his mouth twisted into

an ugly smirk. "Even if you could get away, the authorities would never believe you. Think about it. I'm a hardworking man who was attacked by a deranged woman demanding passage. They'll put you in prison for the rest of your life. And that's a fate far worse than you could ever imagine." He paused. "Now what's it going to be? You're wasting my time. If you won't put down the glass and remove your garments, then I'll rip them from your body." He started toward her.

There was no chance to think…Maggie had to act quickly. As he reached out for her, she swung her arm back and then brought it forward in one quick motion, plunging the shard of glass into his chest. She pushed it until it lodged deep inside, and then backed away from him.

O'Shaunessey's eyes widened, and she watched in horror as he pulled the bloody weapon out of his chest. He staggered and tried to clutch at her, his arms flailing at the empty space. When Brian placed his hands over the gaping wound, blood seeped through his fingers. He looked at her once again and then collapsed in a heap, hitting the floor with a dull thud.

Maggie stood frozen for a few minutes, staring at O'Shaunessey's lifeless body. She expected to feel remorse for what she'd done, but all she felt was relief. Maybe later, when she was safely back with Paddy and it all sank in, she'd face the moral conviction for what she'd done. But right now all she could think about was getting her passage.

Suddenly, a thought struck her. What if someone came looking for O'Shaunessey and found his body? Had anyone seen her with him, or had he told someone? Maggie had to think fast. First, she needed to empty his pockets. She bent down and avoided looking at his face as she searched his pockets. Maggie removed some money and a small book. She hurried to the bed and set the items on it, then looked around. Her passage must be in his coat pocket. She hurried over to where he had tossed his coat and found her ticket, some papers, and the key to the room. Maggie set them on the bed with the book and money.

Even though she would lock the door behind her when she left, she needed to do something with the body in case the owner of the room decided to enter. Maggie glanced around the small room. There was nowhere his massive body could be hidden. She walked back to the corpse. O'Shaunessey's opened eyes seemed to be staring at her. Maggie shivered as she looked away. Her eyes were drawn to the bed. She studied it for a few seconds. It might be tall enough to hide his body.

She had to try. Maggie bent down and began pushing and rolling his body. She stopped several times to wipe the sweat from her brow. Panting and using every ounce of strength she had, she finally reached the bed. She rested for a few seconds and then pushed until she got the body as far under the bed as it would go. Maggie picked up the shard of glass he had pulled out of his chest and threw it next to his body.

A trail of blood followed the path to the bed, and there was a large pool where he had lain. Maggie had to mop it up. She grabbed some dirty clothes, picked up the splintered glass from the bottle, and then tossed it under the bed. Next, she used his coat to mop up the blood as best she could, and then pushed the coat under the bed as well. Maggie turned her head and looked at the dark bloodstain still visible on the floor. She picked up another pile of dirty clothes and dropped them over the stain. She stood back, pleased with her work. Even though the body wasn't visible from where she stood, she walked back to the bed and arranged the bed coverings so that they draped over the edge of the bed to the floor.

Maggie was anxious to get out of the room. She looked

down at her blood-spattered clothing and hurriedly put her cloak on and fastened it. Grabbing the items she'd retrieved from his pockets, she stuffed them securely into the deep pockets of her cloak. She gave the room one more look and then exited, locking the door behind her.

CHAPTER EIGHT

Patrick and Connor stood with slumped shoulders and hands rammed into their pockets in front of Kelley's Pub. Patrick sighed dejectedly as he looked down the street for any sign of Maggie. Why had he let her go? Whatever fate beheld her was his fault, and he knew it would be unforgivable because he'd never find solace for his part in it. He feared that Connor's sisters were lost to him, but he didn't tell him that. Connor needed hope, and by thinking he would find them, it would keep his spirits up.

Connor turned to him. "What was that man talking about, Patrick? Did you understand?"

"I understood," he replied flatly. "We've been swindled. O'Shaunessey never intended to give passage to our sisters." He cleared his throat. "He said they'd be taken care of, but not in the way we or they could ever imagine." He exhaled loudly. "You understand why he asked to see our sisters alone. You know what he intended to do to them. It was no secret. We both knew, and we let them go without a fight. We should have at least fought for them." He swallowed the lump in his throat.

Connor hung his head. "No, I didn't know, Patrick. I was naïve. But now I know." Tears stung his eyes. "My sisters are so young and innocent. I don't want to think of it." He looked at Patrick. "We can go to the authorities."

"It'll do no good," Patrick replied as he picked up the bundle and slung it over his shoulder. "They'll offer no help to us. I know where he took my sister. I hope she's still there. Maybe your sisters are there, too. I need to go before it is too late to save Maggie. He may have already taken her to a secret location." He paused. "Aye…why didn't I think of this before instead of standing here?"

"O'Shaunessey never told me his intentions for my sisters."

"You didn't know what he intended to do to them in exchange for their passage?"

Connor shook his head. "I thought because they were girls they needed special paperwork."

Patrick studied him, surprised at Connor's admission. He hadn't realized O'Shaunessey's real motive. That further saddened Patrick, and he felt sorry for Connor. "How old are your sisters, Connor?"

"Bridgette is a year younger than me…fifteen. And Katie is fourteen." He removed his hands from his pockets. "I'll come with you to find your sister. Perhaps Bridgette and Katie will be there, as you said."

They walked in the direction O'Shaunessey had taken Maggie. As they turned the corner, Patrick was shocked to see Maggie running up the alleyway toward them.

"There she is, Connor. It's Maggie!" he said excitedly. Patrick took off in a sprint toward her. He scooped her up into his arms. "I was so worried," he cried as he released her and then held her at arms' length as he stared into her eyes.

"Are you hurt? Did O'Shaunessey give you your passage?"

"Oh, Paddy! You're a sight for sore eyes. I...I'm fine." She looked behind him and noticed Connor standing looking hopefully at her. "You find a new friend?" she asked her brother.

"Maggie, this is Connor Murphy. O'Shaunessey took his sisters two days ago. He promised them passage. He was to return them, but they never came back. Did you see them?"

"I wish we were meeting under more pleasant circumstances, Connor." She studied his youthful handsome face. She saw the hope in his eyes. "No, Connor. I'm sorry, I didn't see your sisters." Her legs began to weaken, and suddenly she began shaking.

Patrick was alarmed. He held her close. He assumed the realization of what had just taken place flooded her mind. "Are you ill, Maggie?" He didn't want to think about what she had been through. Right now he was just thankful to the Lord that his sister was safely returned to him. He prayed that Connor would have the same reunion very soon.

"No, Paddy. Get me away from here. Hurry! I need to leave this horrible part of town."

"What happened to you, Maggie? Why did O'Shaunessey let you go? Some men told us horrible things about O'Shaunessey. Did you escape?"

"There's no time for talk now, Paddy. Let's go wait by the boats. Tomorrow they'll take us to Dublin. Please. Let us go now."

The three of them walked through the crowds, some huddled together by the boats. A few massive, rugged looking men stood guard near the boats.

Patrick found a spot somewhat secluded from the main body of people. After they settled themselves on the ground, he turned to Maggie. "We can talk privately here. Tell me everything…well, almost everything." His face flushed.

She patted his hand. Her heart was still pounding and she took several deep breaths to calm herself. She was safe. Well, she hoped she was. Her nerves wouldn't be put to rest until they were safely in Dublin. She smiled weakly at Patrick and Connor.

"You can speak freely in front of Connor." He sighed heavily. "I almost forgot. You didn't answer about your passage." His eyes clouded. "You need passage. I won't leave Ireland without you. Just as you refused to leave without me."

Before she could respond, Connor pulled his ticket from his pocket. "I have no need for mine. Take it," he said quietly.

"No, Connor, thank you," Maggie quickly said. "I could never take your passage." She paused. "I have mine. We can all leave together, and the sooner the better."

"O'Shaunessey did give you your passage then?" Patrick asked, surprised.

Connor looked hopefully at her and then at Patrick. "Maybe he gave my sisters theirs too, and they are searching for me as we speak. Maybe they are here somewhere in one of the groups waiting to board a boat in the morning."

"I don't think they're here, Connor," Maggie replied quietly.

"But you got your passage. Maybe they got theirs, too."

She swallowed hard and glanced around herself to be sure no one overheard their conversation. "He didn't freely give it to me," she said in a cracked voice. She bit her trembling lip. "I took it. What have I done, Paddy?" She began sobbing as her prior interaction with O'Shaunessey began to play through her mind.

Patrick patted her back until she brought her emotions

under control. "Where's O'Shaunessey?" He looked around at the groups of people.

"He's not here," she sniffed. "Paddy, you don't know what I've done."

"What did you do, Maggie? Nothing wrong. You only took what was promised you."

"No, Paddy," she whispered. "You don't understand. O'Shaunessey never intended to give me my passage. After he had his way with me, I was to be given to some men who would pay O'Shaunessey for me. Women and girls are no longer safe here, Paddy."

"Then how did you manage to escape him and with your passage, Maggie?" Patrick asked.

She unfastened her cloak and opened it slightly.

His eyes grew wide and his face paled. "Has O'Shaunessey hurt you? All that blood!" His voice trembled as he stared at her bloodstained dress.

"Not to worry. It's not mine. It's his." She swallowed hard and her eyes brimmed with fresh tears.

Patrick stiffened and he glanced around. "He's sure to come after us. We need to be careful not to get on his boat."

"No, he won't come looking for us."

"How can you be certain, Maggie?" her brother asked.

She shuddered as images of what she'd done flashed through her mind. "He's dead," she whispered hoarsely.

"Maggie, what happened? Tell me."

"Paddy, what have I done? I've killed a man! May God have mercy on my soul."

Patrick immediately embraced her. "What choice were you given?" he asked softly as he tried to console her. "God surely knows that and has already forgiven you."

"Is this what I've been brought to, Paddy?" she cried.

"How can God forgive me of such a sin? Have I the right to even seek His forgiveness?"

He held her shoulders and looked into her eyes. "No, listen to me, Maggie. O'Shaunessey brought it to himself. He is…was a vile man. The Lord will see it that way."

Maggie sniffed. "I pray He does, Paddy." She dried her eyes.

Patrick continued to hold her tightly. "I was so afraid I'd never see you again, Maggie. What did O'Shaunessey do to you? Did he —?"

"No," she quickly answered. "I…I couldn't do it, Paddy. I would rather be dead."

"How did you kill him?" he asked in a low voice.

"I…." She stopped and drew a deep breath. She wanted to avoid as many details as possible, even though she knew they would stay embedded in her mind for a long time. Maybe she'd never be able to rid her mind of those vivid images. "I broke a bottle," she said, trying to control her trembling voice. "I took a large jagged piece of the glass…." She broke off, unable to control her emotions, and began to tremble violently. Patrick's arms held her tight. "I was terrified of him. He gave me no choice. Please forgive me, Paddy."

"Nothing to forgive you for," he stated firmly. "I would have done the same. No need to tell me more. You're safe now, Maggie."

Connor had been sitting quietly listening, but now broke his silence. "What if someone finds his body?"

Patrick stiffened for a minute and then relaxed. "No one knows us." He looked at Maggie. His forehead wrinkled. "When it's dark, Maggie, we'll find a place for you to change your dress. We'll hide it somewhere."

"You told those men in the pub that your sister was with

76

him," Connor reminded Patrick.

"I pushed his body under the bed. I pray no one finds it before we're safely on the boat to Dublin," Maggie said. She pulled his room key from her pocket. "I locked his door behind me."

"I'm certain he had many enemies," Connor stated. "No one will know it was you. If they ask Patrick or me, I will say that you are my sister."

"Thank you, Connor," Maggie replied.

He nodded. "You did a good thing killing him. Saved other women and girls from his evil clutches."

"If he didn't have the bottle, I may have not been able to escape."

"Connor and I were coming for you. I'm grateful the bottle was there."

"Aye," Connor replied. He twisted his hands together as he looked into Maggie's eyes. "O'Shaunessey took my sisters. They could be anywhere. Two days ago. His boat may have already taken them to Dublin. Or they could still be here. I don't know what to do. I failed them."

"Connor, I'm so sorry about your sisters. You didn't fail them. You'll stay with Paddy and me. We'll do everything to help you find your sisters. And when we get to America we'll stay together."

He shook his head. "No. I'll stay here. Maybe I'll find them if I keep searching."

"But they could already be on a ship to America. They could be there waiting for you," Patrick reasoned.

Connor placed his head in his hands. "I don't know what to do."

"We'll stay together," Maggie said again. "You'll never be alone, Connor. And I promise you, when we get to America we'll all search for your sisters. We'll never stop until we find them." She reached inside her pocket. She retrieved the book, but left the money safely hidden inside. It was better they didn't know about it in case they needed it later… especially when they reached America. "I took this book from O'Shaunessey's pocket." Her eyes narrowed. "I need to ask the Lord to also forgive me for stealing off a dead man."

"He's stolen more from so many," Patrick said through gritted teeth.

"Maybe this book will hold a clue where your sisters are, Connor," Maggie said. She offered the book to Patrick. "You read it."

Patrick took the book from her and slowly began to flip through the pages. "All these women." He paused and looked at his sister in shock. "Maggie, your name is in here. Next to it is written 'Paid in full by Ian O'Malley for debt owed.' Next to that is written 'Passage for Patrick Quinn if Margaret Quinn is as stated.'"

Maggie's heart froze. "Forgive me, but I am not sorry that he is no longer in this world."

"Neither am I," Patrick said, giving her arm a squeeze.

"Are my sisters' names in that book?" Connor asked.

Maggie saw the tension in his face. Either way it wouldn't be good news for him. Her heart cried for him. He was just a boy not much older than Paddy, and like Paddy had been left as the man of his family. He carried the weight of the world on his shoulders, as Paddy did. She couldn't imagine what was going through Connor's mind.

Patrick continued turning pages and slowly reading the names. "Here they are. Murphy: Bridgette and Katherine."

"That's them," Connor said hoarsely.

"I'm sorry," Patrick said. He patted Connor's shoulder

while Maggie grabbed his hand and held it.

"What's written next to their names, Patrick? Does it say where they are?" he choked.

Patrick looked back at the book. "Says 'Passage was paid to Connor Murphy in exchange for Bridgette and Katherine Murphy.'" He inhaled sharply. "Next to their names is written 'Shipped Out.'"

"No!' Connor cried. "Shipped out to where, Patrick? Does it say?"

Patrick was silent for a few seconds. He looked at his friend. "To Liverpool, England."

Connor covered his face with his hands. "What have I done to my sisters? Why have we been brought to this fate?" he moaned.

"Connor, you've done nothing wrong," Maggie said softly as she moved closer to him. She put an arm around him. "There was nothing you could do. Evil has overtaken our land, as if we hadn't suffered enough with the failure of our crops. Please get on the ship to America with us. Your sisters might be there waiting for you as Paddy said. Possibly they went to Liverpool and will board a different ship there for America." Maggie hoped her words would give him some comfort, even though she doubted O'Shaunessey put them on a ship to America. She knew what their fates had become, and it sickened her. Maggie intended to stay true to her word. She wouldn't give up until Connor learned what became of his sisters.

"Maybe they'll come back here," Connor replied.

"I don't think so, Connor. They've been shipped out. What choice do you have but to go to America? It makes no sense to stay here when they've been shipped out," Patrick explained sympathetically.

"I don't have the strength to go on without them," he cried.

"We're not giving up looking for them, Connor. You have my word," Maggie said emphatically. "The three of us will stay together."

"There's nothing here for any of us now, Connor. We've all lost so much," Patrick said.

"I don't know how to go on without them. We're all that's left of our family."

"Aye, you have more strength than you know, Connor," Maggie said. "Do it for your sisters. You need to stay strong for them." She held him closer. Like Paddy, the survival of his family had been put on his young shoulders. "Connor," she said softly. "They're alive, so there is hope."

He drew a shuddering breath and blinked hard. "I will have to hold on to that. Thank you, Miss Quinn."

"Call me Maggie. I insist."

He nodded. "Patrick is fortunate to have you."

She shook her head. "I am the fortunate one." She smiled at her brother. She could see in his eyes that her comment made him proud. He deserved her praise, and she would continue to be grateful to him for all he'd done, and at such a young age.

Patrick stood and set the bundle holding their possessions next to her. "I still have the coins O'Shaunessey gave me. I'll try to find us some food while you two get acquainted," Patrick said.

Maggie watched him walk to a small wooden lean-to that offered assorted breads and tea to those who could afford it. She turned her attention back to Connor. She noticed that he had no possessions with him. "Have you no change of clothes, Connor?" she asked.

He hung his head. "My bundle was stolen from me my first night in town."

"I'm sorry, Connor." She patted his hand. "Tell me about your sisters," she said softly. "How old are they?"

"Bridgette is fifteen and Katie is fourteen. We had two older brothers, but the fever took them and my ma and da." His shoulders slumped. He looked into her eyes. "Patrick tells me you lost your family to the fever, too."

"Aye." She studied him, noting how thin he was, even thinner than Patrick. "Are you older or younger than Bridgette?" His youthful looking face made his age hard to determine.

"I'm sixteen," he replied. "My brothers were eighteen and twenty." His eyes misted.

She wanted to ask him more about his sisters, but now was not the right time. She looked up when Patrick returned with three chunks of bread and three small tin cups of tea. "It's not much, but will put something in our bellies."

"Thank you, Paddy. This is a feast," Maggie said as she hungrily bit into her bread.

"We'll sleep here tonight, and in the morning we'll get on the boat that will take us to Dublin, then the ship to America. We're safe now," Paddy said.

She hoped they were, but she wouldn't feel at ease until they were far away from here. She prayed no one would go looking for O'Shaunessey until they were safely on the boat. "I won't feel safe, Paddy, until I set my feet on America's soil. I pray to God that soon this wretched life will be behind us." As they ate the rest of their meal in silence, she observed how much calmer Patrick appeared. As others moved past them she warily looked at them, and was fearful that someone would sneak up behind them.

Chapter Nine

Maggie stood between Patrick and Connor among the large group anxiously waiting for their boat assignments. When darkness had fallen last night, she'd moved into the shadows and, guarded by Patrick and Connor, had quickly changed out of her blood-splattered dress and put on a fresh one. After she finished, Patrick had wadded the dress up and walked to where lit barrels were scattered among the groups for some warmth against the chilly night air. He tossed it inside. That made her feel slightly better, but still she'd spent a restless night with little sleep, as had the boys. Every little noise had jarred her nerves. She wondered when their next decent sleep would come.

She hoped America was as wonderful as they'd been led to believe. It had to be. She doubted any of them could take much more. They'd been battered and beaten down by life. None of them asked for much, except honest work for honest pay, decent food, and a warm bed. But most of all safety. She wanted to feel safe again.

She stood looking at the others awaiting their boat assignments, and saw that they didn't seem to be in any better shape than they were. They all had hope in their eyes that the long arduous journey they were about to embark on would restore their souls and give them a decent life.

"Soon we'll be on our way," Patrick said with a cheery note in his voice as he squeezed her hand. "Life will be good again."

She smiled at him, and found her body relaxing slightly until she noticed a large, mean looking man making his way toward them. Her heartbeat quickened. Had someone found O'Shaunessey and seen her with him yesterday? She trembled slightly. The man's eyes scanned the crowd as he walked. He suddenly stopped next to Patrick. As his eyes swept over Patrick, Maggie's breath caught in her throat.

"You look like I know you," the man said in a deep voice.

Patrick looked the man in the eye. "I'm sure we never met, sir," he replied with a puzzled expression on his face.

The man frowned as he scratched his head. His eyes narrowed. "It comes back to me now. You were looking for a friend who was to give you your passage. I see you found him, then."

"Now I remember," Patrick replied. "Yes, I found him and we are waiting to board the boat."

"Have a safe journey." The man nodded and walked off.

Relief flooded through her as the man continued walking through the crowd. But her relief was short lived as a bellowing voice cut through the quiet chattering of the crowd. A man stood by one of the boats. "Where's O'Shaunessey? Anybody seen him?" The man moved toward the front of the boat. "No time to waste," he shouted to another man. "We leave without him. Fill the boats, and I'll get another to take his."

Patrick took Maggie's elbow and leaned down close to her ear. "See, no worries."

"Until I set foot in America I will worry," she replied.

****

After they were settled on the boats cramped together, the rocking boat lulled Maggie to sleep. For that she was grateful. She drifted off as Patrick and Connor talked about their plans in the new country. Maggie awoke as they were discussing what they intended to do with their fortunes. She was pleased to see that they had the hopeful dreams of youth. She couldn't stretch her aching muscles due to the overcrowding, but knew they would soon be arriving in Dublin. Maggie closed her eyes and drifted off again.

"We're here, Maggie," Patrick excitedly exclaimed pointing. He gently shook her shoulder.

Maggie rubbed the sleep from her eyes. "We're in Dublin, Paddy." She grabbed Patrick and Connor's hands. "It'll be good again."

****

They were pleased to learn that their ship would be departing Dublin in the morning. The excitement was contagious between the three of them. "We'll stay here tonight," Paddy said, looking around. "Many others are, too."

"Where else would we go?" Connor asked seriously, and then grinned.

Patrick laughed as he slapped him on the back. "I have some coins left. I'll find us some food and drink while you find a safe place to settle for the night."

Connor nodded and took Maggie's elbow and led her to a reasonably safe area where a few others had settled. "This will be good."

Patrick returned with bread and tea. "This is all we had money for," he apologized. "The fare is much better with meats, but very expensive."

"This will sustain us, Patrick. Someday we will have meat and vegetables again."

"And potatoes, I hope," Connor added.

"Yes, big beautiful potatoes," Maggie said with a laugh in her voice.

****

"This is not what I expected, Paddy," Maggie said quietly as Patrick, Connor, and she were crammed into the lowest level of the ship. She looked around and was shocked at the filthy, cramped conditions. The strong odor was almost unbearable. She felt her stomach lurch, but drew air through her mouth. She couldn't allow herself, or Patrick and Connor, to become ill. They needed to stay strong. Others seemed to have the same reaction, as their faces registered their shock at how they would make the journey jammed together as they were.

"No, but it will be worth it to be free again," Patrick replied.

"I hope we will be, Paddy."

"Aye," a fellow traveler said. "It will be worth it. Some of my family is in America already, but we had to wait." She wrung her hands. "My husband and brother are waiting for us. They have work for me."

Maggie looked at the woman's weathered face. It was hard to determine her age, but three small children clung to her skirts. They were thin and their large eyes peeked from behind their mother at her. "I hope to find work along with my brother and our friend."

The woman's brow furrowed. "Who is meeting you?"

"No one. Patrick and I are all that's left of our family," she explained. She extended a hand. "I'm Maggie Quinn." She pointed to Patrick and Connor, who were chatting with some other passengers. "That is Patrick and Connor."

The woman took her hand. "It's a pleasure to make your acquaintance, Maggie Quinn. I'm Ana O'Sullivan. These three here are Derry, Finn, and Aiden."

"It's my pleasure to meet all of you," Maggie replied. She was happy to have another woman to talk to. It had been so long that she'd had any companionship outside of her mother and Patrick. She was happy that Patrick and Connor were making friends, too. This would be good for all of them. When things got better for Ireland, she vowed to return. No matter how much opportunity America would offer them, her heart would always belong to Ireland, but she would always respect and honor America. As they were shuffled into their quarters, she was happy to learn that Ana O'Sullivan's space was next to theirs. As deplorable as the conditions were, Ana and she could pass the time chatting while the boys became acquainted with those their own age.

Several days into the journey, many of the passengers became ill and Maggie did her best to make them comfortable. When Ana became seasick, Maggie amused the children with Irish songs and tales. At night she held her Bible close to her heart, and prayed that the Lord would see them all safely to this new land.

One night as Maggie sat reading her Bible to Ana, Ana suddenly grabbed her hand. "What is it, Ana?" she asked quietly. "Is there another passage you would like me to read?"

"Promise me something, Maggie," Ana said.

Maggie stared into the woman's frightened eyes. "What is it, Ana?"

"Promise me that if I don't survive the journey, you'll see that Derry, Finn, and Aiden get safely to their da when the ship arrives in America."

"You'll be fine, Ana," Maggie said soothingly. "You'll be reunited with your husband."

"Please promise me."

"I promise," Maggie replied. She was worried about Ana, and fervently prayed for her recovery.

As the days dragged on, several of the passengers succumbed to illness. Maggie cried along with their families and prayed with them at their loss. She kept a close watch on Patrick and Connor. They had to stay well. They were given so little to eat and drink that she was worried it wouldn't be enough to sustain them on this arduous journey. Ana wasn't improving, and Maggie tried to reassure her children that she would be fine, but deep down Maggie feared the worst.

Several days later, Maggie noticed a slight improvement in Ana. Each day she continued to improve. Maggie breathed a sigh of relief.

"I'm happy my sickness has passed," Ana said early one evening as her children slept nearby. "It was told to me that they will not allow sickness."

"What do they do when we arrive?" Maggie asked.

She shook her head. "I do not know." She looked at Maggie. "Do you have papers?"

"Aye. They are in the Bible where they are safe."

"Do you have papers to show someone is waiting for you?"

Maggie lifted an eyebrow. "I do not know what you mean, Ana."

"I don't know if it's true. Just what I heard." She patted Maggie's hand. "Not to worry. Could be rumors."

Later Maggie told Patrick and Connor what Ana had said. "What should we do, Paddy? Do you think they would send us back after what we've been through?"

"Have you heard of this, Connor?" he asked his friend.

Connor shook his head. "I don't know what to expect when we arrive."

Maggie chewed her bottom lip. "We need to be prepared. We can't go back."

Connor laid a gentle hand on her shoulder. "Be calm, Maggie. We've come this far." He was quiet for a minute. "Did O'Shaunessey have any papers with his book?"

Maggie's spirits lifted. "Yes." She patted Connor's cheek. She reached into her cloak and withdrew some papers. The three of them huddled over them.

"Here," Patrick pointed. "Says seamstress. That's you, Maggie." He looked further. "Connor and I can do this one."

Maggie read the paper. "It's good. What type of work is it?"

He shook his head with a smile. "It doesn't matter, now does it, since we won't really be doing it."

She laughed. "No, it doesn't matter, but mine would be true."

"Just getting off this ship and having land beneath our feet and fresh air to breathe instead of this stench will make me happy," Connor said. His eyes clouded. "So many began the journey with us, and so many were lost, never realizing the dream of a new life." He crossed himself.

"It is sad, Connor. We will never forget them."

****

"We're here, Maggie!" Patrick gleefully exclaimed.

Tears streamed down Maggie's face. They'd made it. They were finally in America. "Praise be to God," she said.

Ana came over to her and hugged her. "I hope to see you again, Maggie Quinn. If it weren't for your songs and stories, I don't know how my children and I could have endured the journey." She paused. "And I would not be alive today without you nursing me back to health."

Maggie hugged her back. "We will meet someday again, Ana O'Sullivan. And I shall never forget you, Derry, Finn, and Aiden," she said, stooping to hug each child. "When we meet we'll have a celebration with food and music," she promised.

"We'll never forget you either, Maggie Quinn," Ana said as they disembarked.

As they were led off the ship and the crowd was placed in a line, Maggie made sure each of them had their paperwork ready. "Stay close," she said to Patrick and Connor. She looked around but had lost sight of Ana and her children. Maggie said a silent prayer for their new beginnings in America, as well as their own. She looked around at the other passengers. Most were weak, tired, and hungry. Some appeared very sick. If what Ana had said was true, she doubted they would survive a return journey, and her heart broke for them.

Maggie tried to mask her nervousness when it was her turn to show her papers to the handsome American. He had a kindly face. She wondered if it was difficult to refuse those his work told him to. He looked at her, then down at the documents she'd presented to him. He studied them, and then looked at her for a minute before asking her name.

"Margaret Quinn," she replied calmly.

He wrote her name down and motioned for her to move along. She breathed a sigh of relief as she waited for Patrick and Connor. They came along shortly. Her heart was lighter than it had been for some time. She walked between them and they gazed at the city in amazement.

"We made it, Maggie," Patrick exclaimed. Tears streamed down his cheeks. "Praise God! Our new home is New York City."

"I only wish Bridgette and Katie were here to share this joy with me," Connor said tearfully.

Maggie knew his soul wouldn't rest until he found his sisters. His tears were of both joy and sadness. She squeezed his hand, knowing that no words she spoke would ease his heavy heart.

"Connor, when we have enough money, we will sail to Liverpool and look for them," Patrick promised. "We will find them."

"If that is where they were left, and if they are still alive," he replied.

"First we must look for them here. They could have been brought here, as Maggie said before," Patrick reminded him.

Connor nodded. "I suppose it is true. It was such a hard journey." He sighed. "They might not have survived the trip."

"Connor, you must not think that way," Maggie chided him. "The Lord will watch over them."

They stood quietly for a few minutes looking in amazement at the crowds of people, some well-dressed, others in rags. Several fine buggies passed them by, and some not so fine. They watched as several of their shipmates climbed into some of the buggies.

"This is the land of opportunity!" Patrick shouted. "America will be kind to us. It is different from what we left behind."

"Where shall we go?" Maggie asked as she watched families being reunited and hustling away. "We have no one to meet us and show us where to go."

"Let's walk for a way and maybe someone will offer us help," Patrick replied.

As they began their trek into the unknown, several beggars surrounded them, pleading for food and money.

Maggie was relieved that Patrick and Connor were holding tightly to her arms. She pitied the beggars, seeing the despair in their eyes. But like them, they had nothing to offer. She vowed that someday she'd help as many as she could.

"Is America different, Paddy? It appears to be the same. Has our journey been in vain? Should we have stayed in Ireland? If I am to succumb, I'd rather it be in my beloved Ireland, and not in a foreign land of strangers."

"Pay no mind to those who refuse to work, Maggie. America will pay fair wages for an honest day's work." He breathed deeply and smiled. "Our lives will be good here. This is what our dear departed ma wanted for us. We would surely be dead by now if we'd stayed in Ireland. We would have starved or been consumed by the fever."

Maggie was thoughtful for a minute. "Paddy, maybe these people can't find work. There are so many. Maybe we have been deceived about America, and there is not plentiful work."

Patrick squeezed her arm. "Where's your faith?" he asked. "The Lord will take care of us. Or don't you believe that anymore?"

"If you lose faith, Maggie, how can I believe my sisters will be found?" Connor said.

Maggie didn't want to dampen their spirits, but her heart had sunk if even just a little. She frowned. "You are both right. I need to keep my faith strong."

"You'll feel better once you get a full belly and a proper rest," Patrick said as he continued to look in amazement at the bustling city. "We need to find shelter and food. Better food than what was provided to us on the ship." He made a face.

"Aye. It is a strange land. Will take time to get used to," Connor said.

Maggie wondered how any of them would survive living in a city, especially one this large the likes of she had never seen. Could Patrick, a farmer by trade, condition himself to working in a building instead of out in the rolling green fields with fresh air? Of course she had to remind herself again that it had been some time since Ireland had seen those lush green fields or smelled the freshness of the air. "Where do we go now? From the looks on the faces of some of the others, they are as lost as we," she stated quietly.

They quickly stepped back when two fancy carriages rumbled by too close to where they were walking.

"We can follow some of the others," Patrick decided. "Maybe they will lead us to lodging and food." He adjusted the bundle he'd slung over his shoulder, holding it tighter as they witnessed a group of young boys run past a few travelers and snatch the bundles they'd set on the ground.

They saw a large group who walked ahead of them turn a corner. "We'll follow them," Connor said, looking at Patrick.

Patrick nodded. Before they had reached the corner, a man stepped in front of them, blocking their path.

"Colin Doyle at your service. How can I help you?" he asked with a broad smile and a hand extended to Patrick.

Patrick reluctantly shook his hand and then Doyle offered his hand to Connor, who shook it in kind.

Doyle smiled at Maggie. "No need to be afraid. I offer you no harm."

Maggie studied the well-dressed man. She figured him to be near her age. He was rugged with a sturdy build. He was a handsome man, she had to admit, with dark hair and brown eyes. She straightened her shoulders. "I don't fear you," she said sharply.

"And you are?" he asked with the same friendly smile.

"Margaret Quinn, but I answer to Maggie. This is my brother Patrick," she said, nodding toward Paddy, "and our friend Connor. We've just now arrived from Ireland. If you'll pardon us, we'll be on our way."

"It is an unpleasant journey on the ship. Not enough food or water. No proper rest."

"Aye," Maggie replied. "Now please let us pass."

The man did not attempt to unblock their path. "It seems like only yesterday that I was stepping off the ship. I was tired, hungry, and knew not what America offered me." He swept his hands over his fine clothes. "Now look at me. I never lived such a fine life in Ireland."

Maggie's eyes narrowed. "I'm looking, and I see a braggart."

Patrick tugged her arm. "Maggie, this is not the way to start our new life in America." He looked apologetically at Colin Doyle. "Please forgive my sister."

"Paddy, I have a voice," she replied heatedly as she stared coldly at Doyle. "I am not asking forgiveness for my words."

Colin tipped his hat to her. "Well, then, I apologize if my words offended you, Miss Quinn. I am only trying to show you that America is truly the land where dreams can come true. In my case, they did."

Maggie frowned. "Right now we are weak, tired, and hungry from the journey. Can you direct us to where we might find shelter and food? Tomorrow we will seek work after we are rested."

"I know just the place where you can rest. Maybe I can help you seek employment, too. What work would you hope to find?" he asked.

"Patrick and I are farmers," Connor quickly replied. He looked around himself. "I see no fields, but we have strong backs and will work where we are most useful. Can you tell me where we might find a farmer seeking hands?"

"This is New York City. I fear if you intend to settle here in the city, you will be seeking work of a different nature," he replied to Connor.

"No matter," Patrick cut in. "We are not afraid of any kind of work."

"And I assume you are looking as well?" Colin turned to Maggie with a bright smile.

"I am," she replied. Her instincts told her not to trust him, but she didn't want to believe that his offer of help wasn't genuine. He was taking his own time to offer help. And they did need help. None of them had a clue of what to do or where to go.

"I can help all of you in your search. It may not be glorious work, but it will be honest and enough to pay your expenses."

Maggie's instincts still wouldn't allow her to fully give her trust to him. "And why do you offer your help to strangers? It seems a bit strange," she said.

Colin's eyebrows drew together. "Why are you so bitter, Miss Quinn? Has your heart been hardened against all? I also came from Ireland, as I have said. I know what has happened to our once beautiful land."

Maggie thought about what he had said and knew that his words rang true. She was being unfair, and the last thing Da and Ma would want was for her heart to become hardened. Her features softened as she looked at the stranger. "This time I apologize, Mr. Doyle. It is not easy to know who to give my trust to in these hard times."

"I accept your apology and will explain why I offer help." His face grew serious. "No one was here to offer me help when I stepped off the ship three years ago. By God's grace, I

94

survived living in the streets for months. I found work when I could. It was not enough to secure a bed to rest my head every night. But I didn't give up. I worked hard long hours for anyone who needed my help. The owner of many buildings and businesses in the city stopped by one day. He offered me permanent work." He sighed. "After that day I vowed to help others because the Lord provided so plentifully for me. That is what we should all do. No?"

"How did you make your fortune?" Patrick asked, intrigued.

"There is plenty of work for those willing to work hard. It takes time. Many employers are distrustful of new arrivals. Some of our own, I'm ashamed to say, have done some unspeakable crimes after arriving."

"They deserve to be punished then, as should anyone if they cause harm to another. Does not matter from where they come," Maggie stated without hesitation.

"Their actions did not help new arrivals to be trusted," Colin said.

"We will prove that we are hard workers and honest," Patrick emphatically said.

Maggie pointed to the groups of beggars. "What about them, Mr. Doyle? Why are they begging for money and food if work is plentiful here?" she asked quietly.

Colin sadly shook his head. "Many of them got sick after their arrival and could no longer seek work. Others got sick in their heads, some through drink, and still others are lazy, expecting to come to America and find instant riches without working."

Maggie lifted a skeptical brow. "Where is help for the sick and deranged?"

Colin spread his hands wide. "Would you blame me for

all the woes of the world, or expect an Irish man who was poor upon his arrival to have all the answers?"

"I fear that trust still does not come easily to my sister." Patrick turned his head and eyed Maggie sharply. "Maybe it never will."

Maggie's eyes met her brother's. "May I keep reminding you that I have a tongue and can speak for myself, Patrick?" she replied, and then turned her attention back to Colin. "This is not the America we were told about."

"I fear many have been told wild stories. I felt the same as you when I arrived. My hopes were stepped on and my faith low. But still, I learned it is a land of many opportunities…if you know where to find them."

Connor, who'd stood quietly listening as he shifted his weight from one foot to the other, now spoke. "It is getting late, Mr. Doyle. Could you please show us to a place of shelter? We need food and rest."

"You three be staying together?" Doyle asked.

"Aye," Patrick said, looking again at Maggie. "We must be on our way before we collapse in the street."

"Let me drive you," Colin offered. "My carriage is over here," he said pointing to the opposite side of the street where several carriages were lined up. "Come."

Maggie hesitated.

"If you don't wish my services, there are many others who will accept."

Maggie eyed Patrick and Connor, who nodded their acceptance of Colin Doyle's offer. She turned back to Doyle. "We accept your kind offer."

They walked with him to his carriage and settled into the comfortable seats. Maggie stretched her legs. It felt good to be off her feet for a little while. Doyle's carriage wasn't as fancy as some she had seen, but also wasn't as run down as some others. It was roomy, and she watched as Patrick and Connor also stretched their cramped legs. The expression on Patrick's face was peaceful, but Maggie still had worries. Connor's face told her that he would never fully rest until he learned the fate of his sisters.

"Paddy, all these people," she whispered. "I never thought I'd see so many hungry in America. Maybe some, but not so many."

Patrick exhaled loudly. "We don't know their reasons, Maggie. As Mr. Doyle has said, many are in poor health and not strong enough to work. Maybe they have no family to take them in." He patted her hand. "But we are strong. We will work."

"Aye. I fear it is only our stubbornness which keeps us alive."

"Then it is good," Connor added. "We have plenty of that."

Chapter Ten

They rode the rest of the way in silence. Maggie felt her eyes grow heavy, but she kept them open as rows and rows of buildings and shops passed by. She saw very little green grass. She'd never been in such a large city, and she'd never seen so many buildings and people. As the carriage rode on, she noticed that the buildings became less pleasant looking and seemed to be more crammed together, rising high into the sky. People were out front of the buildings standing around talking, while others sat on the steps as children played nearby. How could she possibly get used to living day after day without sprawling lush meadows and fields of green beneath her feet? But then she was reminded that it had been a long time since she'd seen the greenery of Ireland before they left.

The carriage finally slowed and then stopped. Maggie was dismayed at the run-down building Colin Doyle had stopped in front of. This building was worse than many they'd passed. She looked at Patrick and Connor. Their faces showed their disappointment also.

"It's a place to rest our weary bones," Patrick said.

Maggie sensed he was trying to lift their spirits, but he was right. She was too tired to care at this point. Tomorrow they would seek different lodgings. Things would look better in the morning after a decent night's sleep and some proper food in their bellies.

She squeezed Patrick's hand. "We all need food and rest."

Colin helped her step down from the carriage and the boys followed. "This is it," he said, leading them to the walk in front of the building. "There is a nice flat available," Colin said. The tenants stayed where they were sitting or standing, but flashed bright smiles at them. Maggie smiled back. Their faces looked tired, but happy. Happy just to have a place to live, Maggie thought. It would be nice, though, to have companionship with the women. And it looked like there were several young men the boys could befriend.

"And as you can see, most of these tenants are Irish. You'll be safe here," Colin added in a low voice.

Maggie stopped and looked in surprise at him. "Because we are Irish we may be treated different from others?"

Colin cleared his throat. "Not always, but some don't like to hire Irish. Not all take kindly to strangers entering their land." He looked at Patrick. "Before I take you to the flat I must ask if you have the rent. I will collect it every month on the first day."

"Are you the owner of the building?" Patrick asked skeptically.

Maggie bit her tongue and decided to let Patrick handle the situation. He needed to know that she trusted his judgment. She would step in only if necessary. Right now Patrick needed to feel the pride as head of the family. Her gut feeling about Colin Doyle had been right, though. He'd played a cruel trick on them bringing them here. He didn't offer them help out of the kindness of his heart.

Colin chuckled. "No, Patrick. I rent the flats when they are vacated, and collect the rents every month. Imagine me owning this building."

"Then how do you afford such a fine carriage and clothes?" Connor asked.

"I have a generous employer. He pays me well for renting the flats, collection of the rents, and running his many errands." He gestured toward the entrance. "Now let's take care of the payment and then you can rest."

Patrick's jaw tightened. "We have no money," he stated. He threw his shoulders back proudly as he looked Colin in his eyes. "We will work for some food and a roof over our heads for tonight."

Colin frowned. "Surely you jest. It does not work this way. If you seek only a room for one night, there are many boarding houses. Still you must pay first. It will cost you more to rent a room for a month than renting a flat for a month. I don't know anywhere in the city where you can obtain shelter and food and pay later. There is no one who will offer it to you." He stared hard at Patrick for a full minute, and then at Connor and Maggie. "What is your desire?"

"Then we will be on our way. We will find shelter." Connor rammed his hands into his pockets. "I'm sure of it. Someone will help us," Connor stated confidently.

"Like those at the docks, Connor?" Maggie asked, crestfallen. "Who is helping them?" Maggie knew she had the money she'd taken from Brian O'Shaunessey's pockets to cover the rent and more, but she realized that Colin Doyle only wanted to take advantage of their misfortune. His heart wasn't as kind as he'd led her to believe. She was right not to trust him. Maybe they could find a better place to live. She didn't want to part with any money until she was certain they weren't being taken advantage of. She hoped Patrick wouldn't be upset with her for not telling him about the money.

Patrick's shoulders slightly stooped. "No matter. We have no money. No need taking any more time from Mr. Doyle." He grabbed Maggie's arm. "Not to worry. We'll find shelter."

Colin ran a hand over his jaw. "Before you take your leave," he began, "there is a matter of payment for the carriage ride. You must pay me for transporting you."

Maggie's face flamed and she could control her tongue no longer. 'Sir, you have deceived us," she said angrily. "Shame on you! May God have mercy on you. All you said is lies! You are no better than the thieves in the street. I am right not to freely give my trust." She turned to Patrick and Connor. "We shall be on our way now." She grabbed their arms and tugged them until they began to walk with her down the street.

Colin followed them. "No, wait!" he called. "You need to pay for the carriage ride. Or should I contact the authorities?"

Maggie had to think quickly. If he went to the authorities, it would be found out that they lied about the papers they'd showed at their processing. Her heartbeat quickened and she felt the tension in both Patrick and Connor, who still held tightly to her arms. They stopped and turned to face him. Maggie noticed that the tenants out front of the building were also staring curiously.

"Maybe we can work it out," Colin offered. "If you don't have money, surely you've brought something valuable with you from Ireland. I will take that in exchange for money."

"No. All we have is our clothing. We have no valuables," Patrick replied.

"Hmm. That does present a problem." Colin pulled on his chin.

Maggie's eyes flashed. "There is no problem. We were led to believe you offered your services from a kind heart. You are a cold-hearted cruel man, Colin Doyle. You seek to take advantage of those who have nothing." Her lips tightened. "I hope to never set my eyes on you again," she said through gritted teeth. "Now we will be on our way."

Colin narrowed his eyes as he looked into hers. "Even if I let you go, it's late. Where will you go?" He paused. "Are you sure you have no valuables?" he asked again. "You'll not be safe on the street."

Maggie threw her shoulders back. She looked at Patrick and Connor. They were as exhausted as she. She'd have to pay Colin Doyle the rent. They were in desperate need of food and rest. "I am much too tired and hungry to argue. Lead us to this flat."

"There is no need if you have no money or valuables for payment," Colin said firmly.

"My brother and Connor have no money. You didn't ask me," she said forcefully.

Patrick and Connor looked at her, surprised. "Maggie, this is no time for games."

She held a hand up. "Let me handle this, Paddy. Please?"

He nodded. "If you wish," he said reluctantly, and then looked questioningly at Connor, who shrugged.

"I assumed—" Colin began.

"You assumed that I am a woman incapable of taking care of herself," she said haughtily, eying him distastefully. "I am quite able of speaking for myself and taking care of myself, Mr. Doyle."

"You are an unusual woman, Margaret Quinn. You bring back fond memories of someone I once knew." Colin swallowed hard and then cleared his throat. "If you have

102

enough money the flat will be yours. But the rent will be due on the first day of each month. If you do not pay, you will be evicted immediately."

Maggie studied him. "Why has your heart hardened? Why have you turned your back on the people of Ireland? Have you become so desperate you take advantage of those fleeing our country to come to America?" She placed her hands on her hips and kept her eyes locked with his. "You've sold your soul to the devil, Mr. Doyle!"

"Maggie, that's enough," Patrick said. "Can we do some chores to pay for the carriage ride, Mr. Doyle? We will owe no one. Please don't get the authorities."

"Brother, have you not listened?" Maggie asked exasperated. "Be still. I will pay. Do not beg this man for mercy, because he will offer us none."

"This is not the time for games, Maggie," Patrick pleaded. "We have no money, and you know this to be true."

"I said I will pay and I will," she replied firmly. "Take us to the flat, please."

Colin eyed her warily. "Come this way."

The tenants cleared the steps and watched as they followed Colin into the building. Maggie's eyes swept the stained, dirty walls. Some places were crumbling. There was evidence that someone had tried to clean them. The wooden floor was well worn, but clean. The hallway was dark, with the only light coming from a small window at the end of the hall. A staircase led to the flats on the floors above. There were several doors on either side of the hallways, and Maggie assumed the floors above them held many flats.

"The flat is at the end of the hall," Colin said.

Maggie was relieved that she wouldn't be forced to climb the many stairs to a flat above. As she followed Colin Doyle, she heard the voices of children, singing, and music coming from behind the doors.

Colin stopped in front of a door at the very end of the hall on the left. "Here it is." He opened the door and they stepped into a dark, musty, and very dirty room. He quickly found a lamp and lit it.

Patrick held his nose. "This is worse than what we left," he exclaimed. "The fields of rotted potatoes smelled better than this!"

Maggie walked around the flat, ignoring the odor. She moved to the cooking area and saw possibilities once it was cleaned up. The room contained a wooden table, two benches, and a crude counter with a shelf above it against one wall. A small wood-burning stove for cooking was against the other wall. Walking to the main room, she saw that a fireplace stood against one wall, and there were two large chairs and a small couch. Maggie turned to the dirty window, which overlooked the street, and peered out of it for a few seconds. She could sew some coverings for the couch and window. "Once the flat is washed it won't be so bad. We will get the odor out," she said. She nodded. "It is a roof over our heads. Someday maybe we will live in a finer place, but for now we have no right to complain." She moved away from the window and went to the two doors on the other side of the room. She opened each door and peeked inside. The rooms each contained two mattresses on the floor, but nothing else.

"How much?" Maggie asked, closing the bedroom doors.

Colin pulled a small book from his vest pocket. He turned a few pages, and then walked to Maggie and pointed to a figure written in the book.

Maggie's nose crinkled. "Is too much."

He raised his eyebrows. "You can go elsewhere, but most

charge even more for a flat not as nice as this."

"It is not so nice, but I am too tired to argue. I will pay. When we find work, we will move to a better place, Mr. Doyle."

He frowned at her. "Your wages will never cover much more than the rent and some food…that is, if you can find work. There are many searching, and many more arriving on the ships looking for the same."

"There are three of us. We will find work. We will prove ourselves by working hard." She looked into his eyes, which showed no emotion. "Someday, Mr. Doyle, you may be working for me."

Colin slowly shook his head back and forth with a wide grin on his face. "Such dreams of folly. A man working for a woman." He chuckled. "Now for the rent. If you will be so kind as to pay me, I will take my leave, Miss Quinn. I warn you, if this is a trick to allow you shelter for the night, you will raise my ire."

"Excuse me for a moment, Mr. Doyle," Patrick said. He took Maggie's arm and moved her to the other side of the room out of Colin's hearing range. Connor followed.

"Maggie, what are you doing?" Patrick whispered, deeply agitated. "We can't pay, no matter the price. Playing games with this man will surely anger him. He lies about work and opportunities. If he brings the authorities on us we'll—"

"No, Paddy," Maggie said patting his arm. "I'm no fool to play a game with him." Her forehead narrowed. "I've kept a secret from you. I do have the money."

Patrick was confused. "Where did you get such a large amount of money, Maggie?" he demanded. "It makes no sense.'

Maggie touched his arm. "I am not proud of what I've

done, Paddy. When I took my passage I emptied Brian O'Shaunessey's pockets of all his ill gotten money."

"Why did you not tell me? Why did you let me worry? Knowing this would have given me some peace."

"I know, Paddy, but it was best to keep my secret until we were safely in America. I was afraid it would be stolen from you if anyone saw you had it. But I fear there are as many who would steal from us here, too." She drew a deep breath. "May God forgive me for what I've done in order to come to this country."

Patrick exhaled loudly. He glanced in Colin Doyle's direction. The man stood looking curiously at them. "He will. You turned money made through evil to something good. If Ian O'Malley hadn't deceived us, it would have been different. From this day forward, we will all work hard to make our way honestly in this strange country. I pray that America will be kind to us. May God bless our new life in America."

"Da taught us to work hard, and Ma taught us to never give up. They both taught us to always be proud that we are Irish. Please, Paddy, don't ever forget where we come from," Maggie implored him.

He hugged her. "I never could, nor would I want to."

"Patrick Quinn, you are still the man of the Quinn family." She pulled the money from the pocket of her cloak, counted some out, and handed it to him. She tucked the rest back into her pocket. "Pay Mr. Doyle. I will never take that honor from you. I put in extra for the carriage ride. We will be owing to no one."

"Thank you, Maggie."

"You're a good woman, Maggie Quinn. The Lord has already blessed me by bringing you and Patrick into my life," Connor said as his eyes misted. "Thank you."

Maggie hugged him tightly. "The three of us are now family. Don't you ever forget that," she said with a lump in her throat.

The three of them walked back to where Colin Doyle stood looking out of the window.

"This will cover the rent for the rest of the month and the carriage ride. We will pay the money when next it is due," Patrick said, handing him the money.

Maggie saw the pride on Patrick's face. She would never take that away from him. He'd done more than his share to keep his family alive the past few years, at such a young age. She hoped his life wouldn't be filled with only strife and struggle. He'd never had a chance to enjoy as many good times as she had, and she vowed to make his life happy. He deserved everything good that this life had to offer.

Colin glanced at the money, and then handed some back to him. "The carriage ride is free."

"You said we owe for it," Patrick stated.

Colin nodded. "My employer doesn't charge for transportation if the flat is rented." He tucked the money into the book then placed the book back into his vest pocket.

Patrick studied him. "You could have taken the money for yourself and we would have never known."

"I could have," Colin replied. He looked at Maggie and met her eyes. "I could do many things. I have done many things." He turned back to Patrick. "Be careful, lad. New York City is filled with many like me. But unlike me, they wouldn't walk out the door and leave the rest of your sister's money hidden in her cloak."

Patrick shook Doyle's hand. "I thank you for that, Mr. Doyle. Maybe you are a kind man deep down."

He frowned. "Many would disagree with you."

"Could you be so kind as to tell us where we may find some food, Mr. Doyle?" Maggie asked.

"I will take you to purchase supplies." He held a hand up, palm out. "No charge." A smile broke across his face.

Chapter Eleven

"The money should last for many weeks if we spend wisely," Maggie said as Patrick, Connor, and she sat on the wooden benches at the table finishing their meal.

"Aye. Connor and I will look for work in the morning," Patrick said.

"As will I." She glanced around the room. "Soon we will make this a home. Our home." She smiled.

Patrick nodded. "It will take much work, but it is better than living on the streets as beggars."

"If it weren't for the money, Maggie, we would be on the street instead of here with full bellies and a warm bed tonight," Connor said.

"Connor, no matter our fate, we three will survive because we have the strength of Ireland in our hearts and souls. The Lord has a plan for us. If not, He would have taken us with the fever, too."

Connor finished his sausage and bread and then drained the last of his tea. He got up from the bench and began pacing around the flat while Patrick and Maggie finished their supper.

"This is not the land I was told about," Connor said, coming back to the table and sitting down. "I am discouraged."

Maggie reached across the table and patted his hand. "Nothing worth having ever came without a price. We are still safer here than we would be in Ireland."

Patrick frowned. "You never wanted to leave Ireland, Maggie. Now you say that she has turned on us. Aye?"

She shook her head. "No, Paddy. Ireland will always have my heart. Is not her fault what has happened to her. She will rise again in all of her green beauty. Someday I will go home again when she returns to the land I once knew." She smiled. "Now I will make America my home. And you will seek your fortune, Paddy." She winked at him.

He laughed. "Dreamer."

"There are always possibilities," Connor said. "America is a new chance."

Maggie saw the sadness in his eyes. Though she sensed he was trying to find a way to move on without his sisters, she knew it wouldn't be possible, and she would be there to help him, but she would somehow find a way to learn of their fate and be there to comfort him if the news was sad, or share in his joy if it was good.

"Colin Doyle was kind enough to show us the best places to purchase food," Connor said.

"And there is a church close by," Maggie said. "We haven't been in a long while."

Patrick nodded. "Now we must rest. Tomorrow will be good."

****

Maggie nodded to a few of the women as she made her way out of the building. A pleasant middle-aged woman stopped her. Her hair was bright red, with a smile as bright to match.

"You're the new tenant. I live across the hall." She extended a hand. "I'm Molly O'Brien."

Maggie shook her hand and smiled back at her. "I'm Maggie Quinn. My brother and our friend rented the flat last night. It's a pleasure to meet you."

"If you need to find your way around, I'll be pleased to help," she offered. "As will my husband, Charlie, and our two daughters, Erin and Rose."

"Thank you, Molly. I look forward to meeting your family."

"Tonight then. I need to get to my work. My family has already gone."

Maggie began walking, wishing she were the one that had a job to go to. The boys had left the apartment before her. She was sure they would find something. She didn't know what work would be offered, but she would do anything. Maggie walked into each shop she passed filled with hope, but left discouraged. After several hours, she dejectedly turned toward home. Patrick and Connor would find work. The Lord wouldn't bring them this far to abandon them now.

As she passed the church, she stopped and looked at the beautiful building. She needed solace. It had been so long since she'd been inside a church, and she felt fortunate to have one so close to their new home. Maggie quietly slipped inside. A few parishioners were in several pews praying. She wondered if their prayers were the same as hers. She slipped into a pew and bowed her head. Maggie was praying so fervently, she didn't notice that someone had moved close to her until she lifted her head. She looked into the kindly eyes of an elderly priest.

"Welcome, my child," he said softly.

"Thank you, Father. My family and I will be attending services on Sunday."

"It's always nice to see new faces. I'm Father O'Ryan."

Maggie smiled at his kindly face. "I'm Maggie Quinn."

"I'm glad to know you, Maggie Quinn. Are you newly arrived?" the priest asked.

"Just yesterday. We are seeking work."

"May I pray with you?"

"Aye." She bowed her head as the priest prayed with her. After they finished, she asked him to hear her confession.

On her way out of the church, she took a few coins from her pocket and placed them in the collection box. Even though her heart was heavy due to her lack of finding work, it was lighter because she'd been able to unburden her soul, and also because she'd met Molly O'Brien.

When she opened the door to her flat, she saw that Patrick and Connor were still out. That may be a good sign, she thought as she busied herself preparing supper. She placed a few vegetables in a pot and added the rest of the sausage. While she waited for the boys, she picked up the family Bible from the table, walked to the main room, and sat in a large chair. She opened the Bible and began to read. A few minutes later the door opened and Patrick walked in, followed by Connor. She could tell by the looks on their faces that their news wasn't good.

Patrick walked over to her and dejectedly plopped down on a chair near hers. "We walked till our legs could go no more. There's no work for us."

Maggie set the Bible on a table. "We'll find work, Paddy." She walked to the stove and stirred the stew. "You'll feel better after a hearty supper."

"Smells good," Connor said, moving to a bench.

"Thank you. It'll be ready soon." She set a plate of bread on the table. "I met one of our neighbors this morning," Maggie said brightly. "She'll come visit with her family tonight. Maybe her husband can help us find work."

"It will be good to have friends here," Patrick said, walking to the bench and sitting next to Connor.

"I went to the church and met Father O'Ryan. I told him we will see him on Sunday."

"It's been too long," Patrick said.

"Aye," Connor agreed.

Maggie dished up the stew and said grace. The stew was especially delicious, and she assumed it was because it had been quite some time since they'd had a stew with vegetables and meat. They all ate heartily, talking little, each consumed with their own thoughts.

When she finished eating, Maggie folded her hands and set them on top of the table. "I thought we might clean this place tonight. We can't do every room in one night, of course, but we can do a little each night." She smiled. "I brought my sewing needles, and there is enough money to buy material to make some coverings. Once we find work, we can purchase nice furnishings."

"We will make it shine," Patrick said with a wink.

Maggie was pleased that the meal seemed to have put him in a better mood. Connor was sopping up the last of his stew with some bread. He also seemed happier than he had been.

"We will make it our home," Connor said.

****

Connor was busy washing the window while Patrick washed down the dingy walls. Maggie swept the floors, then dipped a cloth into a bucket of water and scrubbed them.

They were half way through their chores when a light rap sounded on the door.

"That must be Molly," Maggie said, tossing the cloth into the bucket and then hurrying to the door. Patrick and Connor set aside their cloths and slowly walked toward the door. Maggie opened it and was pleased that Molly had come for a visit. And she had brought her family.

"Come in, please," Maggie said cheerfully, ushering them inside. "I apologize it is so messy. We are cleaning the flat."

"We will help," Molly said.

"Oh no, you are our guests."

Molly smiled widely. "No, we are neighbors. Others helped us when we came here." She grabbed her husband's arm. "This is Charlie, and these two are Erin and Rose."

Maggie introduced herself to Molly's husband and daughters, and then introduced Patrick and Connor to the family. "We were fortunate there was a vacant flat," she said.

"Aye," Molly answered. "The family who lived here before you thought the streets would be paved with gold." She chuckled. "They moved on to seek their fortune elsewhere. They didn't want friends with anyone here."

"Their noses were up here," Charlie added, placing his hand above his head.

The group laughed as Molly continued. "The family before them was a pleasant husband and wife, but sickness took them." She blessed herself. "Now show us what needs cleaning."

Maggie knew it did no good to argue with the woman, and she was grateful not only for the help, but for the friendship. She glanced at Patrick and Connor and their expressions told her they felt the same.

Charlie O'Brien had dark hair and was as pleasant as his

114

wife. Maggie instantly liked him, as she had Molly on their first meeting this morning. Their daughters were the same ages as Patrick and Connor. Both were pretty girls. Erin, the elder daughter, had red hair like her mother, and beautiful green eyes. Rose had hair the color of her father's and brown eyes.

They chatted as they cleaned, and when they finished, Maggie offered them cups of tea. They settled around the table and Maggie thanked them again for their help.

"Do you know where we may find work, Mr. O'Brien?" Patrick asked. "Connor and I looked all day."

He frowned. "I'll check at the factory. I load and unload large cartons all day. It doesn't pay much, but helps."

"Thank you," Patrick said.

"I'll check at the hotel to see if there is work for you, Maggie," Molly said. "I keep the rooms clean, and Erin and Rose work in the kitchen. It's not always pleasant work, but it pays for food and shelter."

"We would all be grateful," Maggie said. She observed the family as they chatted. They seemed very happy and relaxed. "Was it hard to get used to America when you first arrived?" she asked.

"Aye," Molly said nodding. "Things are different here. You'll find your way."

"Finding work was the most difficult," Charlie interjected. "But we never gave up. We had to part with some prized valuables, but as long as we have food, shelter, and are all healthy, what more can we ask for? When we believed there was no hope and our money had run out, we found work. The Lord always provides."

"He does," Maggie agreed. "I met Father O'Ryan today. We'll be attending Saint Matthews around the corner beginning this Sunday."

Molly beamed. "That is where we go. We can all go together."

"I'd like that," Maggie said.

"Erin and Rose, why don't you take Patrick and Connor and introduce them to the other lads and lassies in the building?"

Erin's face lit up as she looked at Connor. Rose shyly looked at Patrick. The boys eagerly rose and followed the girls out of the flat.

"Tomorrow I will introduce you to the other tenants," Molly said. "After supper, we like to gather to share friendly talk."

"I look forward to it," Maggie said.

****

The days quickly passed and Maggie and the boys could find no work. Molly and Charlie had tried, but there was nothing available. Every morning the boys still went out looking. Maggie stopped and now spent most of her time sewing. She made several colorful coverings for the windows and tables, and also clothes for the boys and herself.

The church was what gave her peace. So many people were worse off than she was. Maggie spent many hours at the church helping to feed those living in the streets. The shopkeepers brought the church food no longer sellable, but Maggie and the other volunteers turned the discards into soups and stews to hopefully sustain the less fortunate for one more day. She worked tirelessly cleaning the church. She was at peace when she was at church, but even then the doubts would creep in and Father O'Ryan would pray with her. Maggie knew she had a purpose in life, she just didn't know what it was. She'd never worked outside their home before, but knew there must be a skill she was good at. Maggie tried desperately to hold on even when her heart grew heavy. Their money was running low, and each month when Patrick made the rent payment, Colin Doyle made no effort to keep his promise to help them. To be fair, though, they'd never asked him.

But the hours after supper were happy ones, sitting and chatting with the other tenants. Mollie O'Brien and she had become close friends, and she cherished the time they spent together. When she could spare the time after work, Molly helped at the church, as did her daughters. The girls, as well as their father Charlie, proved to be a good distraction from Patrick and Connor's worries. They all had grown to love their flat and their neighbors. She couldn't imagine having to leave. And to add to that worry, they had nowhere to go. They would end up like the beggars who came daily to the church for just a morsel of food.

"Maggie, what will we do?" Patrick asked one night while he frantically paced back and forth. "We have enough money for only this month of rent. What then?"

Maggie's eyebrows drew together. "I don't know, Paddy," she quietly replied. She felt defeated, and she could no longer hide her feelings from Connor and Patrick. "Maybe I can implore Mr. Doyle to give us some time. I was certain we'd find work by this time."

"He hasn't offered to help us find work as he promised," he scoffed. "Maybe he's not as kind as I gave him credit for. I fear his only help will be to throw us on the street. His employer will see to it."

"Have we asked for his help?" she asked sharply as she looked at her brother. Patrick bit his bottom lip, but kept silent. "He'll be here soon to collect the rent. Let me talk to him. Now is not the time for pride."

Connor exhaled loudly. "What good will more time do, Maggie? We still have to pay. Why are we being punished so? What have any of us done to deserve this fate?"

"There has to be work somewhere," Maggie insisted.

"Not in this city. Maybe nowhere in America," Patrick stated.

Maggie twisted her hands together. "Don't give up. Never give up. I will find a way. We've met many good people in America. Don't harden your hearts." Patrick rubbed his chin. "No matter. He will be here soon."

A few minutes later, a loud knock sounded on the door. "It must be him, now," she said. She got up, walked to the door, and pulled it open. "Come in, Mr. Doyle," she said.

"Thank you," Colin Doyle said, and entered the flat. He glanced around and, spotting Patrick and Connor, nodded to them. "Good evening, lads."

"I assume you've come for the rent," Maggie said.

He looked at her with a quizzical look on his face. "Yes, I have. What other reason would I be here?" Colin asked.

Maggie ignored his question. Of course, he'd come for the rent. She didn't know why she'd asked him. She felt foolish. "Paddy, please pay Mr. Doyle."

Patrick stood, pulled the last of the money from his pocket, then walked over to where Colin Doyle stood and handed it to him. He turned his head and looked at his sister for a second before turning back to Doyle. "We will be leaving next month," he said flatly.

"Patrick! We do not know this for certain," Maggie said quickly.

Connor jumped to his feet with a look of pain on his face. "No, Patrick. It is not for sure."

118

Maggie put a hand on Connor's shoulder. She knew it would crush him to leave Erin O'Brien. They'd become very close friends, and spent almost every evening together talking and going for long walks.

Patrick ran a hand through his hair. "This is the last of our money. It's done, Maggie. We came to this wonderful land of opportunity and she has turned her back on us, the same as Ireland. Open your eyes, woman!" he retorted angrily.

"Paddy, this is not so. We've had shelter and food for all these weeks. We need to hold on."

"Dreamer! Your dreams won't fill our bellies or put a roof over our heads. Women earn their keep in a different way. Connor and I need work to provide for our family."

"Are you saying because I am a woman I cannot work? What about women in this building? Or you think I am incapable, Paddy?" Maggie's face reddened with anger. "Would you have me be one of those women who give their favors to men for money? Is that all you believe me to be worthy of?"

"It would give us food and shelter," he retorted angrily.

Connor immediately grabbed Patrick's shoulders. "Patrick Quinn! How dare you speak ill of your sister! It is because of her that we are even here now. Would you rather be back in Ireland? Have you not seen the ships coming in and heard the stories? We are fortunate where many are not. Children are arriving without parents who couldn't survive the journey." He began to tremble. "We have so much to be grateful for."

Patrick's eyes started to narrow and he hung his head for a minute, and then raised his eyes to Maggie. "I'm sorry, Maggie. My words come only from fear. You are capable of working. I would never allow you to work for money from men...." He didn't finish his thought. He cleared his throat and looked at Colin Doyle. "I apologize for my outburst. Our troubles are not yours."

Maggie realized that Patrick's stubbornness wasn't going to allow him to ask Colin Doyle for help. His remark had cut her, but she knew deep down he didn't mean it. He was only frightened, as were Connor and she. She wouldn't ask for help either. Maybe the man wanted them to beg, plead, and then find his amusement in refusing them. She wouldn't give him the satisfaction. "Mr. Doyle, you have the rent. You may take your leave now. As my brother said, our troubles are not yours."

Colin had stood patiently listening, and now he looked at the three of them intently. He did not attempt to leave. "Is it true that your money is gone?" he quietly asked.

Maggie sighed wearily. "It is our business, Mr. Doyle. My brother should not have spoken so freely in front of you. Nor should have I."

Colin looked sympathetically at her. "I may be able to help."

Maggie wondered why he had waited so long to offer his promised help. Now she wouldn't give him the satisfaction. "No, thank you. There is no work in this large city. We will journey to another town if we must."

He looked intently at her. "Where will you go? Surely you don't expect to walk. It's impossible." He motioned to the table. "May I sit?"

"As you can see, Mr. Doyle, we are in no mood for visitors. We have heavy hearts and much to discuss among ourselves."

"Please. I'd like to help."

"Why now? You owe us nothing," Maggie replied coldly.

Colin took a seat without being invited. "I offered help

if you needed it, but you never asked. Each month the rent payment was made. We had no conversations between us, so I do not know of your troubles."

Maggie didn't want to admit to him that he was right, but he was. Still, she didn't respond, but instead decided to let him say his piece. She joined him at the table, followed by Patrick and Connor, who looked quizzically at her. Like her, they kept their silence.

"You are good tenants. You made the flat comfortable."

"Thank you," Maggie replied with the same coldness in her voice.

Colin studied her. "I told you long ago that you reminded me of someone I once knew. I wasn't always the man you see before you today. I was the same as you." He lifted an eyebrow. "I escaped Ireland to come to a better life in America. When I arrived, it wasn't what I had imagined. I became very bitter and discouraged." He frowned. "I will tell you my story if you allow it."

Maggie looked at Patrick and Connor, who shrugged. She took that as them letting her make the decision. "I will allow it," she said.

"I was fortunate to meet a very wealthy businessman who took pity on me one night. It was a stormy and very cold night. He gave me shelter in the basement of one of his buildings. The room wasn't much, but it was better than the streets. In return for his generosity, I was to rent the vacant flats and collect the monthly rents for him. He owns many buildings, shops, and pubs in the city." He paused. "He bought me two suits of clothes and gave me a fine carriage to use to go to the docks when the ships came in. He pays me well for renting and collecting the rents."

"But it worked out well for you. You have work and

shelter," Patrick reminded him.

He nodded, and then clasped his hands together and placed them on top of the table. "But I have sold my soul. My family would be ashamed of me, and rightly so. I'm a tormented man. In the beginning I did what I was told, but then I wanted more than my pay. I became greedy." He drew a shuddering breath. "I robbed the new arrivals of their valuables, and brought them to the flats knowing they were being robbed twice, because the rents were much higher than they should be or what my employer set as the price."

Maggie was deeply disturbed by his admission. She eyed him carefully. "How those new arrivals must have felt being swindled by their own kind. But then they did not know, and like us, knew they had to pay what was asked. What choice was there?" She ran a hand through her hair. "What you've done is not to be proud of, but it is not up to me to judge." She set her jaw firmly. "Your judgment will come when this life is done."

Patrick and Connor looked at Colin Doyle disdainfully. Patrick's features hardened, and Connor kept balling and unballing his fists.

"I'm not proud of what I've done," Colin admitted. "I accept my judgment." He cleared his throat. "I was a bitter, lonely man when I arrived. My family, all of them, were dead from the fever." His eyes lowered and he looked at his hands. "The worst was losing my wife and newborn son on the journey to America." He raised his eyes, which now were tear-filled. "Still, it's no excuse for my unkind deeds. I make no excuses for myself."

Maggie's own eyes brimmed as she listened to him. How horrible to leave Ireland with your wife and child and have them not survive. How must he have felt upon his arrival?

It didn't excuse what he had done, but her compassion for his loss overwhelmed her. She patted his hand. "I'm sorry for your losses, Mr. Doyle."

"Thank you," he said softly as he composed himself. "I have a favor to ask of all of you."

Maggie noticed that he was looking at her. In fact, he hadn't taken his eyes off her. She looked at the boys, who were both seemingly ready to let her answer for all of them. "What is it?" she asked.

"Would you please call me by my given name? And I would be pleased if I could call you by yours." He kept his eyes locked with Maggie's.

"Are you this friendly with all the tenants?" she asked.

"No, but I am going to change. I'm not perfect...far from it."

Maggie wanted to believe he was being sincere, but if she didn't give him a chance to prove himself she would never know. "You may call us by our given names."

"Thank you...Maggie." He smiled weakly. "I would like to continue if I might."

"I would like to hear the rest," Patrick said.

"Aye," Connor agreed.

Colin looked at Maggie and waited for her response. She nodded.

He drew a deep breath. "As I said, I had nothing and I didn't care what I did or who I hurt. When I was offered the employment, my heart rejoiced. I would no more be hungry and cold. But my bitterness remained." He shook his head. "Those that departed the ships with loved ones in tow made me want to force them to suffer as I was suffering. They still had their families. Mine was taken from me."

"You didn't care about the suffering the families were

escaping from and enduring to get to a better life," Patrick said bitterly.

"Many still suffering," Connor added with narrowed eyes.

"And that was your intention when you saw us. You would rob us if we had valuables," Patrick stated.

Colin's eyes clouded. "I'm ashamed to say, but yes, I would have taken them and denied you ever possessed them. New in a strange land, what could you do? The law would offer you no help."

Connor frowned. "Why didn't you rob us then? You knew Maggie had money tucked away."

"Maybe he was afraid of you and me, Connor," Patrick replied. "Is that it?"

"No," Colin answered. "The truth is, it is because of you, Maggie Quinn." His eyes locked with hers.

Maggie saw the pain in his dark eyes. "Me? I don't understand."

His eyes misted. "You reminded me of my beautiful wife; same red hair, feisty manner, and stubborn determination. I couldn't cause you any harm. It was as though my dearly departed wife was standing right in front of me warning me to be kind to you."

"But still you *thought* about stealing from us," Maggie said quietly. She was angry at how he'd treated others, but was sympathetic to his losses. She was torn. She wanted to despise him but couldn't.

"I did. I'm not proud to admit this." He cleared his throat. "I know you suffered much, too."

"Aye. We all have. And we will suffer more if we don't find work. As you know, we have no money left." She smiled faintly. "But we do still have a month to find work." She hoped that now Colin Doyle would offer his assistance.

Patrick suddenly slammed his fist on the table, startling all of them. "Maggie! Open your eyes. We've been searching day after day for weeks. A month now will make no difference. No one will hire us. Half the tenants in this building are without work, and may soon be on the street. We share our stories night after night. They have been here longer than we. Dreaming of a better life won't make it happen."

"Paddy, don't lose faith. The Lord would not bring us this far to abandon us," Maggie said. But she knew her brother's words were the truth. New faces filled the church food line every time Maggie went to help. Father O'Ryan stretched what little food was on the shelves and what was given to the church to feed them all, but she knew that soon that would not be enough.

Connor nodded emphatically. "I agree with you, Patrick. Maggie, praying for it will not always make it so."

"Since you won't ask, I would like to offer my help," Colin said.

"For what price?" Patrick asked bitterly. "You tell a good tale, but I see no sorrow for what you stole from others, only for your own losses."

Colin's eyebrows drew together. "I don't blame you for not trusting me. No price." He looked at Maggie. "Do you sew?"

She laughed. "What woman doesn't?"

"Wealthy women," he stated with an amused smile.

"Why do you ask?" She looked skeptically at him.

"A thought has occurred to me." He shifted his weight on the bench. "The man I work for has a wife who pays big prices for her dresses and gowns. She has no one here to make them to her standards, and her husband complains to me that he has to send abroad for them. It is a concern when the fittings are not right. Do you understand what I'm saying?"

Maggie nodded. "It would be difficult without proper measuring."

"Could you make a dress or gown I could show her? She would be pleased to have a seamstress in the city."

Maggie was thoughtful for a moment. "Even if I agreed to sew her a dress, I have no money for the materials. And if I had the money, it is much too risky to spend it on something that may or may not produce money for my family," she said warily.

He pulled on his chin. "If she will provide the materials will you make a gown? Something very fancy that I can show her?"

Maggie placed her elbow on the table and propped her chin in her hand as she thought about his odd request. "Only if Paddy and Connor find work so that I would be able to sew the gown. We three need to keep looking for work to pay the rent and buy food. My brother does tell the truth. My dreams won't provide food and shelter."

He smiled. "You drive a hard bargain, Maggie Quinn. I promised help, and I will prove I am a man of my word."

"I will be forever in your debt, Colin, if you can find work for me and my friend Connor," Patrick said hopefully.

Maggie was relieved that he had calmed down. This was the first time in months that she had seen hope in Patrick's eyes. Their lives would change and they could enjoy life once again. It had been so long since they'd truly been happy. Sometimes she worried she wouldn't know how to be. Life was strange, and she had learned long ago not to set her stock on things staying the same. She'd never dreamed she'd be living in a country other than Ireland. She never dreamed most of her family would be gone. Many days she sat wishing time had stood still, if only for a little longer. She would be back running in the fields with her brothers and sisters. Da would be playing the fiddle while Ma sang.

Patrick nervously cleared his throat and continued, "I am the man of the house and need to provide for us. It is not my sister's duty to supply the money."

"These are different times, Paddy," Maggie replied. "This is a different country. As long as expenses are paid, no need to worry who pays."

"What would our work be?" Connor asked excitedly. "Provided you find us work."

"I will talk to my employer. Some work is not pleasant, but it's honest work and pays a fair wage."

Patrick grinned. "No matter what the work is. It is work."

"I will return tomorrow evening. We will celebrate with music and dancing."

Chapter Twelve

"Colin should have been here by now," Patrick said impatiently as he peered out the window and then came back to the table.

Maggie sat quietly. Would Colin do this to them? Would he be so cruel? Her heart told her no. He gave his word. If he broke it, she didn't think she'd ever trust anyone again. She doubted the boys would either. They'd been sitting at the table for two hours. As each minute passed, her heart sunk a little lower, but she had to believe he would come.

"He's not coming. We've been made fools of. A wasted day we should have been looking for work." Patrick slapped his forehead. "I should have known. He's likely sitting in a pub laughing about what fools we are. We *are* fools, Maggie. Fools to believe a dishonest man."

Connor sighed. "He appeared to care about our well-being. I believed him. I pray he doesn't prove me wrong."

"You've become bitter young men. Have you no faith or trust in anyone? It is still early. Give him time. He will return."

Patrick exhaled loudly. "It is you, sister, who always says trust does not come easy. But yet you choose to trust this man. I will trust when I have proof. I say Colin Doyle can't be trusted."

"He could have robbed us, but he didn't," Maggie reminded him, meeting his eyes. "Think on that."

"No. He wants something more valuable from us than money."

Maggie laughed. "And what would that be, dear brother, since we have nothing of value?"

"Are you blind, Maggie? Do you not see his intentions?" He looked at Connor. "Connor, surely you do."

Connor nodded. "Aye. He's sweet on you, Maggie. I see it in his eyes every month when he picks up the rent payment. Mostly last night. Maybe that's why he shows such kindness to you. Would he show the same kindness to another?"

"First you say he won't offer anything to us, then you say he will because of me? Which is it?" Maggie's face flushed. "This is foolish talk. His intentions for me are only those of a friend. Could be the disgraceful way he lived his life since his arrival here is causing his shame. Nothing more. We must remember he's suffered as have we."

"Aye. Maybe." Connor winked at her. "Time will tell his true intentions."

Patrick squared his shoulders. "I will never approve of Colin Doyle to court you, Maggie."

"No need. Colin and I will go no further than friendship." She got up from the bench and then placed her hands on her hips, and with narrowed eyes stared into Patrick's. "When I meet a man I care to marry, I will do so with or without your approval, Patrick Quinn. I have my own mind."

Patrick shook his head and was about to speak, but before he could, a knock sounded on the door.

Maggie lifted an eyebrow. "It must be Colin. It is too

late for any other visitor. He kept his word." She walked to the door to open it. "Come in, Colin," she said with a smile, ushering him inside where he immediately unloaded several bundles and a fiddle onto the table after greeting her.

He beamed as he smiled at them. "Tonight we will celebrate! There is much good news I bring."

Patrick picked up the fiddle case. "May I look at it?" he asked Colin.

"Of course."

Patrick removed the fiddle from its case and ran his hands gently over it, admiring every detail.

"Do you play?' Colin asked.

Patrick set the fiddle back in its case. "Long ago. In happier times."

Colin gave Patrick a friendly slap on the back. "Times will be happy again, Patrick."

He exhaled loudly. "Maybe for some."

Colin began to slowly untie the bundles. When he finished, he displayed an assortment of sewing needles, scissors, threads, assorted ribbons, baubles, and some of the most beautiful fabrics Maggie had ever laid eyes on.

"Can you make a gown out of this material and these baubles? I will retrieve whatever else may be needed."

Maggie ran her fingers gently over the rich fabric. "The material is beautiful," she murmured. "I believe I can make an exquisite gown. What size of woman is she? I will need to measure her." She blushed as his eyes swept over her.

"About your size. A little fuller through the middle. Maybe an inch shorter."

"I'll need to meet with her to make sure I get the right size."

Colin bit his bottom lip. "It is to be a surprise for her."

"Hmmm. We wouldn't want to spoil the surprise, now would we?" she asked gleefully. "I can't wait to start. I will begin first thing in the morning." She frowned. "I almost forgot. I will only begin work on the gown if you have secured work for Patrick and Connor. If not, I must continue my search for work along with them."

Colin beamed as he gazed at her. "I have." He turned to Patrick and Connor. "I have. I mentioned that the man I work for owns many properties. He owns a pub right around the corner from here. You two will work there."

"We'll be serving those that come in?" Connor asked.

He shook his head. "No. Your jobs will be to keep the floors swept, windows clean, unload crates, and run errands."

Patrick grabbed Colin's hand and pumped it up and down. "Thank you!" he choked. "You've saved us." He thumped Connor on the back. "Now it's good."

"Aye," Connor said with tear filled eyes.

"Now we can celebrate," Colin announced.

Maggie's eyes filled. "Thank you, Colin. I haven't seen my brother smile a real smile in a long time. You're the answer to our prayers. I don't know how we'll ever be able to repay your kindness."

"No need for thanks." He took her arm. "Would you honor me with a dance?"

"I'd like that," she said with a smile.

"Patrick, can you play a cheerful tune?" Colin asked.

He nodded, then picked up the fiddle and began to play a lively tune. Connor sat in a chair, tapping his foot to the music while Colin and Maggie danced.

****

Molly sipped her tea. "I'm pleased you won't have to leave, Maggie."

"I've grown to love it here. I never thought it possible."

The older woman patted her hand. "I felt the same way. Someday I'll go back to visit Ireland when things are better."

"Do you think you'll ever move back, Molly?"

She sighed. "No. This is my home now. But Ireland will always be in my heart."

Maggie sat contemplating what her friend said. She had to ask herself the same question. She'd go back for a visit, but she, too, had come to love America, even though Ireland would always have her heart. But she'd made a life here, and even though they'd had a rough start, she'd come to truly love the country. "Yes. I feel the same."

Molly's eyes drifted to the gown as Maggie's fingers nimbly worked the sewing needle. "That will be beautiful when you finish. Ah, must be nice to afford gowns such as that."

Maggie looked at her. "Now Molly, how silly would we look in our flats wearing such elegant gowns?" She laughed.

Molly joined her laughter. She silently finished her tea. "Patrick and Connor looked happy when I saw them tonight."

"They are." She lifted an eyebrow. "I suppose Connor and Erin have gone for a walk."

Molly nodded. "That they did."

Maggie smiled wryly. "I think it is more than friendship. Has Erin spoken of it?"

The woman sighed. "She is being coy with her family, but Connor is a fine man."

"That he is. Patrick is fond of Charlie. Is he with him again this evening?"

"Yes. They are entertaining the tenants with the fiddle."

Maggie set her sewing needles down. "I could use some fresh air. Let's join them."

****

Maggie and Molly smiled at Patrick and Charlie, who seemed to be having a contest as each took a turn playing a tune and their captive audience cheered when they finished. She looked around and saw Connor and Erin standing close in the shadows. She smiled, reaffirming her vow to find out the fate of his sisters, Bridgette and Katie.

She breathed deeply. It was good to see so much happiness. She was enjoying the music and the warm night. Life was good...for now.

Molly nudged her. "Look who's coming. Wonder what he's doing here. All rents are paid."

Maggie looked in the direction of Molly's gaze and was surprised to see Colin Doyle walking toward her. She didn't see his carriage and supposed he'd parked it around the corner.

He had a friendly smile as he approached the women.

"Good evening, ladies," he said, tipping his hat.

Molly looked uncomfortably at him, but he quickly put her at ease. Maggie hoped he wasn't here to tell her that his employer had changed his mind about the gown.

"I'm here to see how the boys got along with their work," he said.

Molly's face relaxed. "Good evening, Mr. Doyle. If you'll excuse me, I need to see what my Rose is up to," she said, leaving Maggie alone with the man.

"Good evening, Colin," Maggie said. "As you can see, Patrick is full of joy."

"He's a good fiddle player."

"That he is," she said proudly. "My da taught him."

"And Connor?"

She pointed in the direction where he still stood with Erin.

Colin smiled brightly. "It's good to see such happiness here."

"But they still fear your arrival," Maggie reminded him.

"They aren't comfortable with my appearance," he said with a touch of sadness in his voice.

"I'm certain Molly will let them know why you are here." It suddenly hit her how lonely he was. He had no one to share his free hours with. Her heart softened toward him. He had helped her family, and now there was a way she could repay some of his kindness. Friendship and family were more valuable than all the money in the world. The boys would approve of her decision to include him in their lives as a new friend.

"Colin, do you go to church?"

He looked uncomfortably at her. "I must admit that I blamed God for my misfortune."

"Maybe it's time you gave Him another chance. I'd like you to join us this Sunday morning. We worship at Saint Matthew's. It is not far from here. Most of the tenants go there."

His eyes brightened. "Thank you. I would be pleased to join you."

"After, I would be pleased if you join Patrick, Connor, and me for Sunday dinner." She watched his face. His eyes lit up like a child at Christmas.

CHAPTER THIRTEEN

Maggie sat contentedly, putting the finishing touch on a dress. As she examined it, she was pleased. She thought about the many changes that had taken place in just a few short months. It was hard to imagine how frightened they'd been. It seemed like a lifetime ago now.

She looked around their home. They'd managed to add some new and used furnishings, and it was comfortable and cozy.

She looked up when the door opened. Patrick entered, followed by Connor. "Food will be ready soon," she said. "How was your day?"

"So pleased to be working." Connor beamed.

Patrick swiped a hand across his brow. "It's good to have some money in my pocket. It's nice to have a purpose in this life." He walked over to her and kissed her cheek.

"We've been fortunate. There are so many with nothing. I try to give what I can and to help Father O'Ryan at the church. Colin is also helping very much."

"We have been fortunate, but we worked hard for it, too. Don't forget that, Maggie. Nothing has come easy to us."

Connor nodded. "That is true." He looked at the dress Maggie had finished. "Very pretty."

"Thank you, Connor." She wondered if he was picturing Erin in it. She definitely would look beautiful.

Patrick motioned toward the table, where the two benches had now been replaced by chairs, and noticed it was set for four. "We're having a visitor for supper?"

"Yes. Colin will be joining us tonight. He stopped by earlier to bring more material." She sighed. "He has no one to share his meals with."

Patrick lifted an eyebrow. "Every Sunday, and now during the week, too." He looked curiously at her. "You are taken with him now?" Maggie felt the heat creep up her neck and into her face. "No. He has proved himself a valued friend. Nothing more. Must I keep reminding you of that?" she asked lightly.

Patrick scrutinized her. "Your lips say one thing and your eyes another." He grinned. "You could do worse. You have made an honest man of him, Maggie. Now I will give my blessing."

Maggie tossed her hair. "I will only marry when I feel love in my heart. Colin is not a man of high morals, but I see a kindness in him he hides from others. Still, as I've said before, brother, it will be my decision when and who I marry."

Patrick pulled up a chair and sat facing her. "Maggie, I don't want you to be alone for the rest of your life. You used to speak of having a house full of children." He paused. "You're not so young now."

"Trying to marry me off, Patrick?" She chuckled. "I'm not so old either."

He shook his head. "No. I don't want you to give up your dreams because of me."

136

Maggie grabbed Patrick's hands and held them. "Paddy, that will never happen. I'm not the same woman I was in Ireland. You are not the same lad, but we are family. If I someday choose to marry or not, you will always have a home with me for as long as you want it. My dreams have now changed, but they are still my dreams. I am capable of so much more than I realized." She paused. "You're so young, but have been burdened with a man's duty these past few years. My dream is for you to be happy and enjoy some of your youth. When the day comes that you take a wife, she will be a very lucky woman to have you, Patrick Quinn."

"Marry?" He made a distasteful face. "Not for a long time. I've never thought of any other girl since Meg Kennedy." His eyes lowered. "I still sometimes think of her."

Maggie's mind suddenly filled with old memories and people who'd been in their lives before the bad times fell. She'd been so focused on herself that she hadn't considered the losses, outside of family, that Paddy had also endured. "Our lives changed quickly in Ireland...too quickly. Living here in America for several months now with enough money to pay our way is something we thought was only a dream. Someday I want to do more for those suffering."

"You've a kind heart, Maggie. Do you tell me the truth about marriage, or are you afraid to marry because of your past with Billy McGuire and then Ian O'Malley?"

"How do you remember Billy? You were just a wee lad."

"I heard Ma and Da whispering about him. I'm sorry I don't really remember him...just his name. He was your first love. Da gave him his blessing for your hand in marriage."

Maggie's eyes misted as old memories continued to flood her mind. "I'm not afraid to marry, Paddy. My heart was broken when Billy was murdered." She drew a shaky breath.

"Yes, he was my first love. It took a long time to heal my heart. Then I met Ian. It was not the same kind of love I felt for Billy. They were different in many ways. Billy was a good man. Ian deceived me. I hope to never set eyes on Ian O'Malley again." She cleared her throat. "I never mentioned Billy's name after his death because the pain of losing him was too much for my heart to bear."

"Billy was foolish to pull a weapon on an Englishman. He knew better," Patrick said quietly as he met her gaze. "I heard gossip in town."

Maggie looked intently at him. Her brow furrowed. "Did the gossips say his weapon was a broom? The Englishmen stormed his house, and Billy believed they would do harm to his family. He would have done anything to protect them, but in the end, he gave his life."

"They were being evicted. Billy knew they had to leave. He should have gone when he was told. If he had, he may still be alive."

She nodded. "What you say is true, but he was a proud man. He tried to stand up to the English for the wrongs they were doing to the Irish people of the land."

Patrick slowly shook his head back and forth. "And what good did it do him? Dead he was of no use to his family. Now they're all gone too, just like Meg and her family."

Maggie's tears fell freely and wet her cheeks. "So many family and friends gone, Paddy. My heart breaks. It seems like a lifetime ago now. But we will never forget them."

"Damned English," Patrick spat out bitterly. "They're to blame. They took our land, then the land was blighted."

"As horrible as they are, they didn't cause the potato crops to fail, Paddy. We never knew why that happened."

"But they came and took all that was ours. How many of

138

our women were forced to marry them just to survive? Just so their families could survive? Think how different your life would now be, Maggie, if you'd married an Englishman. You would have never suffered hunger or cold. There was one who was sweet on you. I remember him coming to the cottage quite often."

Maggie made a face and shuddered. "I remember. He was an old, balding, fat man. I was repulsed by the sight of him."

Patrick laughed. "Aye. He was. How did Da keep him away from you?"

Maggie joined his laughter. "Told him I'd been stricken with the fever. He never came back."

He grew serious. "Da was a fine man. I'm sorry for speaking ill of him in the past. I'm deeply ashamed. He worked hard to the end to take care of all of us."

Maggie looked sympathetically at her brother. "You didn't mean it, Paddy. I know that Da, in heaven, is looking down and sees what a fine young man you've grown to be. Da would be proud of you. You are the last Quinn man, and you will be the one to carry on the Quinn name for our family."

"Do you think some of our Irish women that married Englishmen came to love them? Do you think the men were all bad? Is it possible that some of them were good men in their hearts?"

"Are you thinking of Meg?" she asked softly.

Patrick sighed. "It was easier to think of her dead. I wonder what her life is like. Her da wasn't as kind as ours. Now she lives with a man two times her age who, if I am to believe the talk, beats her and shows no love."

"I don't know, Paddy. Meg has most likely learned to survive. I'm certain some of the Englishmen truly do love their Irish wives. I don't think all are bad."

139

"Meg didn't want to leave her family to marry him. She told me she feared him. She tried to hide every time he came around."

"Remember that Meg was one of those who married to help her family," she said gently. "Even if her father forced her into it." She frowned. "I had considered it when things worsened for us. It was months after Da saved me from the fat Englishman. I even spoke of it to Da. He stopped me. He knew it wouldn't be for love, but only survival, and he said a marriage without love would be a terrible fate that he would never want any of his children to endure. He wanted us all to be happy, like he and Ma were. And to be married in our church as he and Ma were." She bit her bottom lip. "Sometimes I think that maybe I should have, Paddy. If I had, then maybe we would still have our land and Ma, Da, and our brothers and sisters with us. Some days my soul is burdened with these questions."

"No, Maggie. Da was right. You've suffered much for our family. If you had married an Englishman, then Da surely would have died of a broken heart."

Maggie looked at the dress she'd made. They'd been through so much, but it was time to finally put the past behind them. The future ahead was bright and filled with so many possibilities. She looked at Patrick and flashed a bright smile. "Enough of this talk. We need to look forward to the future. The past is done. Let's agree to talk no more of it. Instead, let's be thankful to the Lord for what we have today." She held up the dress she had completed. "What do you think?"

His eyed showed his approval. "Your dresses are finer than many I see fancy women wearing."

"Thank you. Colin will be picking it up tonight. Do you mind him sharing supper with us?"

"Of course not," Patrick said with a wide smile. "I've grown very fond of him."

"He enjoys being with us. I think he is a lonely man. He's been here longer than us, but he never took the time to make friends...only enemies. Now he sees that good friends are more valuable than wealth. He is working hard to be the fine man he claims he once was in Ireland. And seeing the change in him, I believe he speaks the truth."

"I believe you had much to do with the change in him, dear sister. He has proved to me to be a decent man. Maybe he, too, yearns for the old days back home. Sometimes I dream at night that we are back in Ireland. Back before the bad times came. It is hard to think of the future when these dreams haunt my rest."

"We're all still homesick for the Ireland we knew, Paddy. Someday we shall see her again. We will take a trip home before we depart this earth. But now, America is our home. Remember, you and I are survivors. The Quinn name must go on. And it will in America. And we will teach our children and grandchildren about the Ireland we knew and to always be proud of where they came from."

"Does this mean you are ready to call this strange land home, Maggie? Irish men are still not treated as well here as others are."

"Paddy, don't blame America. The people here know no better. We are strangers. Someday they will accept us."

Patrick lifted an eyebrow. "But so many of our own have forgotten Ireland, and denounce their heritage so others won't know. Colin treated our people, his people, deplorably upon their arrival. It is a disgrace. I'm pleased for his change. He knows his error. Inside he is still a proud Irishman."

Maggie listened thoughtfully. "Don't forget, Paddy, that

many of our people in Ireland treated their own poorly, too. Let's not forget what Brian O'Shaunessey has done."

"You're right, Maggie."

"I believe that Colin knows he will answer to the Lord when his life is ended. I praise the Lord that Colin mended his evil ways. There is much we had to learn about our own selves since these hard times have come to us. I will answer to the Lord for what I have done, too."

Patrick grimaced. "Maggie, you did what you had to do to defend yourself. If it weren't for you, I don't think Connor or I would have survived the long journey on the ship. There were so many that you helped on that ship. Your singing and cheerful stories kept hope alive when we didn't think we could go on."

"I pray the Lord sees it that way, but sin is sin. Now, we've decided to speak no more of the past. We will look to the future. Agreed?"

"Agreed." He smiled. "Those times are behind us now. No more needs to be said."

Maggie glanced toward the window, where Connor stood staring out at the street. "He is very quiet tonight. Is he not well, Paddy? Did something happen at the pub to upset him?"

"He was fine until he met with an old neighbor of his. He has barely spoken a word since. I fear he is carrying a heavy burden. He cannot move away from the past. Not yet. Hopefully soon. If you had been lost to O'Shaunessey, I would feel the same."

She rose, moved to him and hugged him tightly. "I'm safe...we're together." She nodded in Connor's direction. "I will talk to him."

Connor turned from the window as she approached.

Maggie saw the pain in his eyes. She laid a gentle hand on his shoulder. "Connor, you are so pale. Are you unwell?" Whatever the neighbor had told him had taken the life out of him. She wouldn't push him, but hoped he would share whatever troubling news he had received. "Would you like some tea?"

He shook his head. "No, thank you. I'm well, just yearning to be back in Ireland when I was a lad, before the English came, before the crops failed, and all my family...." He broke off when his voice cracked. "I don't believe I can go on, Maggie."

She knew there were no words she could say to ease his heart, but she had to try. It was obvious that he'd had news about his sisters. It was bad, she sensed. "Connor, you will go on. You must. We have each other, and even though we've all suffered much, your suffering is worse not knowing the fate of your dear sisters." She touched his cheek. "Patrick and I were just talking. We're all homesick for the Ireland we knew. We can keep our happy memories, but we need to leave the bad ones behind. They do us no good to dwell on them. What's done is done. It can't be changed."

Connor's shoulders slumped. "I feel I am betraying everything I stand for...betraying Ireland, my family, if I don't keep remembering."

"Then remember the good times. You're not betraying your family by finding some happiness. They'd want you to be happy and not suffering any longer." She led him to a chair. "Sit." She pulled up another chair for herself. "Paddy tells me you met an old friend today; has he brought you news to cause such a heavy heart?"

Connor covered his face with his hands and began to sob. Maggie instantly was at his side. She wrapped her arms

143

around him until his gut wrenching sobs subsided.

"I'm sorry," he said, embarrassed.

"You did nothing wrong, Connor. What has caused you such pain?" Maggie asked gently. His sobbing unnerved her. He was a broken man, and it frightened her because she didn't know how to console him except with words. Words that she knew sounded empty to someone in the throes of grief.

He dabbed at his eyes. "My friend brought me news of my sisters Bridgette and Katie. It was not good news."

Maggie swallowed the lump that rose in her throat. She didn't want to ask, but she had to know. "Are they...?"

"No," he quickly replied. "They are alive and apparently well. He saw them in Liverpool. He had to wait there for his ship."

Maggie's eyes widened. "Why the tears, Connor? They're alive! That's good news. Are they on their way to America?" She clapped her hands together. "We should celebrate! We can ask the O'Briens to join us."

"No, Maggie, stop," he said hoarsely. "The news he brought to me was not all good. That they are alive and well is good." He drew a ragged breath. "He had a chance to speak with them. They are not the same girls he remembered. He was ashamed to tell me, but I already knew if they weren't dead they were—"

"But you said they are alive," Maggie cut in. She knew what had happened to them. The same life Brian O'Shaunessey had planned for her. Her heart sank. They were so young. She couldn't begin to know the rage boiling inside of Connor, mixed with his sorrow. She didn't know how he kept his two warring emotions under control. Was he blaming his sisters for a fate they had no power over? If that was what was bothering him she had to convince him it was wrong thinking.

"You know Brian O'Shaunessey lied and deceived you, as he did me. It's not their fault. Please don't blame them, Connor."

His eyes filled with fresh tears. "I don't blame them. I blame myself for letting them go with that vile man."

"But they're alive! Why aren't you happy?" She grabbed his hands. "Is there more? What else has your heart so burdened?"

He cleared his throat and rubbed his forehead. "My friend asked them if they would come to America if he could find them a way. He was willing to sell his valuables to secure passage for them. He would have done anything to get them out of Liverpool." He sniffed. "They refused. They told him they were happy in England."

Maggie frowned. That made no sense to her. They couldn't want to continue that unmoral way of life. Something was off. "There must be a reason they would refuse his generous offer, Connor. Maybe they are afraid of the man who is forcing them to—"

"No!" Connor interrupted, shaking his head vigorously back and forth. "I tried to convince myself that this was true, but my friend observed them as they played up to some wealthy men exiting the ships. It's true what they told him. They enjoy the life they found in Liverpool. They eat good food and dress in the finest clothes. They've sold their souls to the devil," he said, defeated. "They give their bodies to men in return for money. They seek nothing more from this life. They chose this path. No longer will I go to the docks looking for them. They never planned to come."

"I'm sorry, Connor," Maggie said quietly. She paused. "I still feel it could be possible they were playacting in front of your friend out of fear. Did you tell him how they became lost to you?"

145

"I should have, but I was ashamed." He wrung his hands. "I suppose they could be playacting, but my heart is doubtful. Someday when I have enough money, I will go to Liverpool and see for myself. If it is an act, I will know and bring them here." He blinked. "It was easier on my heart when I had accepted they were dead."

Maggie didn't believe for one minute that Connor's sisters had chosen, and preferred to stay in, that unsavory lifestyle. She would only believe it if she talked to them herself. That was impossible, but she had to find a way. "Always remember, Connor, that we three are family, and when your sisters eventually come here, because I give you my word we'll find a way, they will be family, too." She touched his cheek gently with her fingertips. "Please don't keep your burdens to yourself. If you are troubled, then it also troubles Paddy and me."

He swallowed hard. "Thank you, Maggie. I'll remember." He hugged her.

CHAPTER FOURTEEN

"Mrs. Beckham wore the gown you made her to a very important party last week, Maggie. Her friends were green with envy, she says." Colin smiled. "She is impressed with how quickly you work."

"I'm pleased she liked it," Maggie replied. "But she paid me too much. More than I deserve."

"No, Maggie. You deserve every penny and much more for your dressmaking skills."

Maggie blushed as she rose from the table. She began clearing the plates.

"I have news. Very good news." Colin beamed as he leaned back in his chair.

"Connor and I will clear the table," Patrick offered with a wink to Connor as he took the dishes from Maggie.

"Are you sure?" Maggie asked.

"We're sure," Connor answered, and then grinned as he stood.

"What is it, Colin?" she asked, reseating herself across from him. "We already have been given so much more than we could ever hope for."

Colin placed his elbows on the table and leaned forward. "If it interests you, Maggie, Mrs. Beckham requests your presence at her home the day after tomorrow. Several of her friends want to employ your services to make dresses and gowns for them."

Maggie couldn't believe the news. She placed the back of her hand on her forehead. "Colin, thank you for all that you've done for us. Of course I will meet with her and her friends," she excitedly replied." She looked around the flat and frowned. "The flat is not large enough for all the materials I will need to make several garments."

"Not to worry. If you are in agreement, Mrs. Beckham will discuss that with you." He turned to Patrick, who had returned to the table with Connor. "Now Patrick, how about some music?"

****

Patrick grinned as he picked up Colin's fiddle and began to play a lively tune. He continued to smile as he watched his sister and Colin dance. Connor watched them for a few minutes, and then slipped away to his bedroom. Patrick was surprised that he wasn't going to spend the evening with Erin O'Brien as he usually did. But Connor's mind was too burdened for company, even if it was the girl he loved. That much he had confided to Patrick. Even if he hadn't, it was evident to anyone who saw the couple together.

He'd overheard bits and pieces of his conversation with Maggie. He wondered why Connor hadn't confided in him, but then realized due to the sensitive nature he was embarrassed. Patrick felt sorry for him, but more sorry for Connor's sisters. He shuddered thinking what could have happened to Maggie if she hadn't escaped O'Shaunessey's grasp. Sometimes he still woke in a cold clammy sweat, feeling as though a claw was digging at his heart. So he could imagine how horrible it was for Connor. He only wished there was something he could do for him. He thought of Connor as a brother. Maybe blood didn't bind them, but circumstances certainly had. They were as much of a family as if they'd had the same parents.

Patrick was happy. He enjoyed his work. He'd met Mr. Beckham on a few occasions, and he was nothing like Patrick had thought the man would be. The man paid fair wages, and the work wasn't backbreaking. In the evening he enjoyed the camaraderie with the other tenants in the building. Most attended Saint Matthews on Sundays, and they all helped out at the church when time permitted. Father O'Ryan appreciated all the help they gave through their deeds, or monetarily. Patrick had never thought they'd have money enough to put in the collection box, and it felt good that they could contribute like their family had in the past. His faith had been restored, and he didn't worry about where their next meal would come from. Maggie was right. He would just think about the good times from the past and no longer dwell on the bad. Life was good. They'd been blessed with more than they could ever dream possible.

As he continued to play, his thoughts drifted to Rose O'Brien. He was becoming very fond of her, but wasn't sure how she felt about him. He didn't confide his feelings to anyone, but suspected they might be aware. She was always nearby when her father and Patrick played the fiddle, and was a captive audience, clapping her hands and dancing around. He didn't want to admit to anyone that he was too shy to ask her to be more than friends, because he was terrified of what her answer might be. On their many walks and talks she'd never mentioned being sweet on any other boy, but she never let him know how she truly felt about him either. But they had become very good friends. He was happy that the Quinns and O'Briens had become close.

****

When the tune ended, Maggie wiped her brow. "That's one of my favorites, Paddy," she breathlessly said.

"I know," he replied with a grin.

"Where's Connor?" she asked, looking at the empty chair he'd been sitting in. "Did he go to visit Erin?"

"No. He went off to bed." Patrick frowned. "He hasn't been himself since his friend talked to him. Did he tell you what was troubling him, Maggie? I overhead some. Is it his sisters?"

She nodded. "Yes, Paddy. The news was about his sisters."

"I didn't know he has sisters," Colin said surprised. "Did they not survive the journey?"

"They survived," Maggie said quietly. "It is much more disturbing. More than his heart can bear."

"Is there anything I can do to help?" Colin offered.

"No one can help, I fear," Patrick replied with a heavy sigh.

Colin was thoughtful for a moment. "Nothing is impossible. There might be something I can do."

Maggie yearned to unburden her heart to Colin, but was torn. Maybe he could help, but by telling him would she be betraying Connor? She wrestled with her conscience. Connor hadn't sworn her to secrecy. In the end, she decided if there was anything Colin could do to reunite Connor with his sisters, it was worth the ire Connor may have toward her. He would realize, in the end, that her intentions were only for his good.

She folded her hands together and placed them on the top of the table, where they had all reseated themselves after the

150

dance. "I shouldn't be sharing Connor's private worries, but you've become a very good friend to us, Colin. If he didn't share with you, Paddy, it's because he finds it difficult to share with anyone. But since my outcome could have been the same, he told me."

Patrick's eyes lowered in recognition of what she was talking about. "I understand."

She drew a deep breath. "I don't think he'll mind if I speak of it now." She paused. "His friend saw his sisters in Liverpool. They don't want to come to America."

"I don't believe it," Patrick stated flatly.

"Neither do I. I believe they say it out of fear." She paused. "He talks as though he is shamed by them."

"It's not their fault." Patrick's eyes narrowed. "He must know that."

"If he sees them I think he will understand."

Colin sat listening intently. "Have the three of you always been close?"

"We only met Connor a little before the ship sailed," Patrick answered. "Our meeting was not under pleasant circumstances. Maggie and I have agreed to put those unpleasant times behind us."

Colin nodded. "I won't pry, but I would still like to offer any assistance that I can."

"You've shared your past with us, Colin. It is only fair that we share ours with you. Then we will speak of it no more, as Paddy and I have agreed."

Patrick nodded his consent.

"Only if you want to," Colin said.

"We do. Then you will truly know us." They spent the next hour sipping tea as Maggie and Patrick told Colin about their family, how they came to know Connor, and what had happened to Connor's sisters. When they finished, Colin sat looking at them with a pained look on his face, but said nothing for several minutes. Finally he spoke. "I feel sorry for myself when others have suffered tragedies maybe worse. I cannot imagine your fear, Maggie, and now the fear of Connor's sisters. Now I understand the sadness in his eyes even when he appears happy."

"No matter the cause of suffering, Colin, the pain is the same for all of us, but your suffering is worse. Paddy and I still have one another, and Connor's sisters are alive." Maggie knew the loss of his wife and child would always leave a hole in his heart that would never be made quite whole.

"Do you know where Ian O'Malley is? Is he in the city?"

Maggie witnessed a flash of anger come into his eyes.

"Better not be in this city if he knows what's good for him," Patrick said bitterly.

"I have no idea where he is," Maggie said. "I assume that when he arrived in America he sold our ma's ring."

"I'll never forgive myself for giving it to him," Patrick admitted.

"Stop, Paddy." She squeezed her brother's hand. "Lives are more important than valuables. We still managed to get here. Now didn't we?" He nodded. "We're putting all of that behind us now, Paddy. We did not know Ian's deceitful plan."

"You're right," Patrick replied. "But if I ever see him, I won't be held responsible for my actions."

"When you escaped O'Shaunessey, Maggie, were you not afraid he'd search for you?" Colin asked.

Maggie's lips drew taut. "No likelihood of that." She drew a deep breath. "He's dead." She held a hand up. "No need to ask how. I will answer on judgment day. It's between the Lord and me."

Colin studied her carefully. "We've all done things to survive that we may not be proud of, but in your case, Maggie, what choice were you given?"

****

Maggie stared in awe at the Beckham home. She had never seen such an exquisite dwelling. The home was a three story white structure located in the wealthier part of the city. A part of the city that Maggie hadn't even known existed until today. Large white columns adorned the front of the house.

"Look at all these beautiful flowers and the green grass!" Maggie exclaimed. A pang of nostalgia tugged at her. It had been so long since she'd seen such green grass and an abundance of flowers. Her eyes sparkled and a wide smile broke over her face. "Imagine living in such a wonderful place. I never saw a house so large."

"Come," Colin said. He handed off the carriage to a young man not much older than Patrick.

Maggie took a few steps and then suddenly stopped. She looked down at her plain dress.

Colin took her arm. "You look very nice, Maggie."

He led her up the steps to a massive porch. Her nerves were ragged. She felt out of place. She tried to calm herself while Colin rapped on the heavy door.

The door was opened by a man about Maggie's age with dark hair, dressed in impeccable white jacket and trousers. She wondered how he kept his clothes so crisp and clean.

He ushered them inside. "Mrs. Beckham is expecting you. Please come this way."

Maggie and Colin followed the man down an elaborately decorated hall filled with paintings on the walls and tables that held statutes and vases filled with fresh flowers. The scent of the flowers was like nectar to Maggie, and she breathed in deeply.

The man finally stopped in front of a door. He tapped lightly and then opened the door and held it wide for them to pass through.

"Come," Colin said. "Don't be nervous," he whispered close to her ear.

Maggie self-consciously entered the room, where several women sat on colorful couches chatting quietly. She again was awestruck at the furnishings. Her eyes were drawn to a beautiful chandelier handing from the ceiling in the center of the room. The women stopped talking and turned their attention to her. She clung tightly to Colin's arm.

"Please, come in," a curvy, very attractive blonde haired woman in her late thirties said. "I finally get to meet Maggie Quinn," she said, followed by a wide friendly smile. "I'm Blanche Beckham."

"The pleasure is all mine, Mrs. Beckham," Maggie replied. She smiled self-consciously as she nervously made her way, still clinging to Colin's arm, to where the woman sat in a large chair covered in a beautiful blue fabric. Maggie noticed that the woman was wearing one of the dresses Maggie had made for her. The woman's warm smile should have put her at ease, but it didn't. She wasn't sure if her nerves came from being in this wealthy home surrounded by all of these affluent women, or the fact that she felt plain and inadequate. The stares of the women burned into her back as she stood before Blanche Beckham.

"May I offer you something?" the woman graciously asked. "Coffee or tea?" She motioned to a plate of small fancy cakes sitting on a large platter placed on a serving cart. "Please help yourself to some cakes. They're simply delicious. Cook made them fresh this morning."

"No, thank you, Mrs. Beckham," Maggie replied uneasily. The cakes looked tempting, and if she were with Molly she would have enjoyed them. But she was out of place here, and her body refused to relax.

"If you change your mind, help yourself," she said with the same bright smile. "Please sit, Maggie."

Maggie looked to where the woman pointed at an empty spot on a couch facing her chair. She moved stiffly to the couch and sat down. Colin stayed standing, and she looked up expectantly at him. Would he be staying for the meeting? She hoped so, if for nothing more than to make her feel surer of herself.

"Colin," Mrs. Beckham began, "Mr. Beckham would like you to take care of a few things. He's left a list with Mary. You will find her in the kitchen."

"Yes, Mrs. Beckham. What time shall I return for Miss Quinn?"

"Give us two hours, Colin. If we need more time I'll let Mary know."

"Very well," he said. He nodded at Maggie and left the room, leaving her alone with these strangers who were all staring at her. Their eyes were friendly and she wished she could relax, but couldn't. She held her hands tightly together and placed them on her lap.

Mrs. Beckham turned her full attention on Maggie. "The gown and dresses you made for me are beautiful! Comparable to, if not better than, the gowns and dresses I've had made in France."

"Thank you," Maggie replied, feeling a slight blush creep into her face.

Blanche Beckham sipped at her coffee, and then set her cup on a table next to her chair. "When my husband and Colin brought the first gown you made to me, I was speechless at its beauty and design. Colin informed me that you are a close friend of his and rent one of our flats. I was skeptical at first, not believing that you had actually made the gown with your own two hands, but my husband assured me you had. Colin had brought the first gown to him and he was impressed, and knew I would be thrilled when I saw it."

Maggie was confused. "I thought the gown was your idea."

"Oh no, dear. You must have misunderstood. There are many seamstresses in the city, some even well known, so I would have no knowledge of your abilities unless you had already established yourself," Blanche answered kindly. "If I'd known you could design and sew such elaborate gowns and dresses, I would have personally asked you." She smiled again. "Let's get down to business. The reason I asked Colin to bring you to me is because I'd like to ask you, since you've made several dresses for me and I've considered you my personal seamstress, is if you'd also be willing to make gowns and dresses for my friends." She swept a hand towards the women, who'd sat quietly listening to the exchange. "They've been badgering me for the opportunity to meet the woman responsible for these exquisite dresses."

One of the women, plump and pleasant faced, excitedly shook Maggie's hand. "It's a delight to meet you. Please say you'll make me a dress. No one in the world has such beautiful designs. And it amazes me how quickly you work." She motioned toward Mrs. Beckham. "It's not fair for Blanche to be the only belle of the ball," she said in a teasing tone, with a sideway glance at Blanche Beckham.

Before Maggie could respond, another woman with jet black hair, slim and pretty, eagerly said, "We'll pay you handsomely. No matter the price."

Maggie beamed, feeling her nervousness leave her. "I will be honored to make dresses for all of you that want them. But I'm afraid my flat is much too small for all the materials I'll require."

"No need to worry about that, my dear. My husband owns several buildings, and I know of at least two that are vacant. One will be cleaned up and supplied with everything you'll need." She grinned. "I'll hire some girls to sweep up and help you with anything you may need."

A sudden thought came to Maggie. "May I ask if it would be possible for a friend of mine and her daughters to be hired to take care of those tasks?"

"Of course. Hire as many women and girls as you need. We'll discuss their pay as soon as the building is ready." She rose. "Now I insist you try those cakes while I pour you a cup of tea. Or would you prefer coffee?" she asked.

"Tea, thank you," Maggie said, as she also rose and retrieved a cake. She couldn't wait to tell Molly about what had happened. Molly, Erin, and Rose would be thrilled with the opportunity, too. Even though they had work, she knew it didn't pay well, and their employer often treated them harshly. No one who worked with her would ever be subjected to belittling treatment or be refused fair pay.

As she sat sipping her tea and eating the delicious cake, Blanche Beckham chatted with her and introduced her to the other women, and soon she felt relaxed. When her cup was drained and the cake eaten, Mrs. Beckham rose.

"Now, shall we begin discussing the kinds of dresses and gowns everyone would like?"

Maggie stood, smiling as the women surrounded her.

CHAPTER FIFTEEN

"I can't believe all that's happened in the last six months," Maggie said. "The Lord has truly blessed us." She swept her arms around the flat, which was freshly painted and was decorated with new furnishings. The old furniture had been given away to those less fortunate, and the bedrooms were furnished with beds, dressers, and wardrobes for their clothes. In the cooking area the shelves were stocked with plenty of food. Two small couches, tables, and comfortable large chairs made a cozy sitting area, while the eating area contained a large table with six chairs with fabric seat coverings. "Still, I was happy with the old furniture," she said. She smiled at Patrick and Connor, who had taken the comfortable chairs, while Colin and she sat on the couches facing one another.

"Maggie, you could have a fine house if you wanted it. The flat is very nice, but why do you choose to stay here when you can now afford so much more?"

"Why waste money, Colin?" She shrugged. "We're happy here, and have made very good friends. We have more than enough for our own needs, and shelter so beautiful sometimes I think I'm dreaming."

"Pays to be a dreamer," Patrick said sheepishly.

Maggie laughed. "Yes it does, Paddy, and don't forget it."

"Aye. It's good not to worry so much. Now we have enough so we can help others," Patrick said.

"Yes. We have more money to help the church. Father O'Ryan is able to feed many more who have nothing." She looked at Colin. "And Father O'Ryan has told me of your generosity."

Colin smiled weakly. "I told you I was a changed man. And I do look forward to attending service with you each Sunday." He looked at her. "Money doesn't buy happiness, but it helps so many who have nothing."

"And Mr. Beckham has donated one of his buildings to shelter and feed many of the homeless. It is because of you."

"No, all the good that has happened is because of you, Maggie. You bring out the best in people. The Beckhams are changed. Mrs. Beckham has grown very fond of you."

"She is a kind, generous woman," Maggie said.

Connor stood. "I've promised Erin a walk."

Patrick winked. "Mustn't keep her waiting.'

"Run along, Connor."

"I think it's serious," Maggie observed after Connor had gone.

"I think so," Patrick agreed.

Colin eyed Maggie carefully. "Are you truly happy, Maggie? Is there nothing more you want from life?"

"I have a peace I never believed I'd know again." She paused. "Colin, there is something I need to know."

"Ask me anything. I have no secrets from you."

She drew a deep breath. "You paid for the materials for the first gown I made for Mrs. Beckham. She knew nothing of it until it was finished and you brought it to her. Why did you not tell me you used your own money?"

His face flushed. "It all worked out."

Maggie's forehead wrinkled. "What if it hadn't? What if I'd made an unsatisfactory gown?"

He thought about it for a minute. "That never occurred to me. But if that had happened, I would have asked Mrs. Beckham if there was a position available for you in her home."

"You are a good man, Colin Doyle," she said warmly. "You are the one with the kind heart."

He spread his hands wide. "The man I am today is because of you, Maggie Quinn."

Maggie rose. "And now I have a gift for my dear brother."

"For me?" Patrick asked surprised. "It's not Christmas or my birthday."

"No matter," she replied. "I'll return in a moment." She went to her bedroom and came back with a large box, which she handed to Patrick. She stood next to where he sat.

Patrick opened the box and sat staring at what was inside.

"Do you like it, Paddy?" Maggie asked softly.

Patrick lifted a brand new fiddle from the box. He turned it over in his hands for a few seconds and then gently set it back into the box, stood, and threw his arms around his sister. "I don't know what to say," he choked.

Maggie beamed. "Is not necessary to say anything, Paddy. Now play something for us."

"Thank you, Maggie," he said tearfully. He picked the fiddle back out of the box and spent a few minutes tuning it. He then slowly began playing an old Irish tune.

"I've heard talk from Mrs. Beckham's cook that she's considering opening a dress shop. She hopes to display your dresses, Maggie. Then you'll be even busier making dresses for women from all over the city."

Maggie's eyes widened. "I've not heard a word."

"I'm sure you will very soon." He nodded as he studied her. "Someday, Maggie Quinn, everyone will know your name. Your dresses and gowns will be worn by women all over the world." He grinned. "You'll be rich beyond your dreams."

Maggie laughed. "I never sought after fame and fortune… just enough for food and shelter. And that I have. As I said, the extra I will use for those less fortunate."

His brow furrowed. "It is fine to have some extras for yourself too, Maggie."

She shook her head. "I have everything I could ever want right here."

He looked intently at her. "Will you ever marry?"

Maggie thought about his question. She thought it odd that he would ask her that. She hadn't even considered the possibility of marriage due to her busy work. She knew that someday Patrick and Connor would take wives and move to their own homes. She never considered how she would feel being all alone when that day came. But then, with the many friends she'd made, she'd only be alone of her own choosing. She gazed into Colin's kind eyes and sighed. "I used to believe I would. It was expected. Now I have a choice."

Colin nervously cleared his throat. "Would you ever consider marriage to me?"

Maggie took his hand and held it tenderly. "I won't marry in the near future, and yes, I will consider you. But I fear you will be long happily married with many children before that day comes. You will make a fine husband to some woman, Colin Doyle."

"I will wait forever for you, Maggie Quinn."

Chapter Sixteen

Maggie sat next to Blanche Beckham in her carriage as they traveled through the city to the wealthier section. She was captivated with the beautiful structures and the abundance of shops as they entered the business district. Women in fancy dresses strolled on the arms of men dressed in suits as they stopped to look in shop windows.

Finally the carriage stopped in front of a large shop. The driver helped them out of the carriage and Mrs. Beckham walked to the front of the shop, unlocked the door, and opened it. "Here we are," she announced.

Maggie followed her inside. Her mouth fell open at the elaborately adorned shop decorated with expensive rugs, paintings on the walls, full-length mirrors, racks to hold the many dresses, and several chairs for the shoppers. One wall was lined with several changing rooms.

"Women can come to the shop to be measured, and at the same time pick out their fabrics and decorations. They can then place their orders and pay a deposit." She paused. "If you take your time and materials to custom make a dress and they change their mind, then the deposit will cover a portion of your time," Blanche explained. "It's good business sense. I've learned a lot from my husband." She chuckled. "The dress shop was my husband's idea. He's gifted with a keen sense when it comes to business."

Maggie nodded. She didn't know what to say, but Blanche didn't seem to require an answer as she continued showing her around the shop and explaining the various features.

Blanche turned to her and stopped talking. She excitedly clasped her hands together. "I've had a brilliant idea and Mr. Beckham agrees. We will hire several seamstresses who, under your tutelage, will sew dresses and gowns. You will give your final approval on them. Gowns and dresses designed and sewed exclusively by you alone will be special order only." She smiled.

"It sounds wonderful," Maggie replied, noting the joy in Blanche Beckham's speech and the twinkle in her eye.

"Of course, Maggie, I still want you to personally make all of my dresses and gowns."

"I feel I am dreaming," Maggie murmured as she took in everything Blanche Beckham was saying.

"I have another surprise for you." She grabbed Maggie's hands. "The shop will be called Maggie's. The sign is being made as we speak. Do you approve?" she asked expectantly.

"I am at a loss for words, except to thank you for all you've done for me and my family." Her eyes filled with tears. Nothing she could say would convey her deepest feelings and thanks for what Mr. and Mrs. Beckham had done for her.

"This is only the beginning, Maggie. You will have full control of the shop and all the workers. Forty percent ownership of the shop is yours. As soon as you are established in the world of fashion, you will take full ownership. It is my gift to you, Maggie Quinn."

"It is too generous. What have I done to deserve this?" she asked, stunned.

Blanche led her to two of the chairs. "I've not always been a kind or generous woman, Maggie, I'm ashamed to admit. My husband and I took advantage of so many to make our fortune." Her eyes clouded. "Watching how hard you, Patrick, and Connor have worked these past two years since your arrival, just happy to have food on the table and a home, has made my husband and me ashamed of ourselves. Colin speaks highly of you and your generosity and help to those less fortunate. You are a remarkable woman."

"Thank you for your kind words," Maggie replied, embarrassed by the praise and surprised that Colin spoke about her to his employer. "I only do what my ma and da taught and raised me to do."

"All should have been taught by parents such as yours. Mine weren't so kind and caring of others' misfortunes, I'm sad to say. Money meant more to them than people, including their children."

Maggie didn't know what to say. Her heart hurt for Blanche Beckham. She couldn't imagine having parents so cold and uncaring.

Blanche continued without expecting a response from Maggie. "But you've made me see the world in a different way. Mr. Beckham and I have more than we'll ever need in ten lifetimes. We weren't fortunate to be blessed with children, so I suppose all our businesses became like our children. I know that makes no sense." She grew serious. "My husband and I are opening a home for the children who have arrived in America without family or loved ones to take care of them. Of course, the home will also house all children in the country who have lost their families. We are also opening a home for the men, women, and children who have no food and shelter. We will help them to find work, and then homes of their own."

Maggie's hand few to her mouth, "That is such good news," she said tearfully. "Everything is good then."

"Everything is good," she replied with a wide smile. "Now let's get down to the details. As I said, you will hire seamstresses of your own choosing, and will be in charge of their work. There are several rooms in the back, which I'll show you in a minute, where the seamstresses will work. I'm having everything moved here from the building you started out in, and of course, adding much more. The seamstresses will be well paid, more than they are currently earning."

Maggie's head was spinning with everything Mrs. Beckham was saying, but she wondered how everyone, including herself, would be able to get back and forth. None of them owned a horse and carriage. Everything they needed was in walking distance from their flats, but this was much too far.

"Is something wrong, Maggie? You look distressed," she asked, concerned.

Maggie flashed a weak smile. "No, everything is wonderful." Her brow creased. "I was just wondering how everyone, myself included, would get to and from work."

She shook her head. "I'm sorry. I should have explained that. My husband and I will be providing transportation. Everyone will be picked up in the morning and returned home in the evening. All that will be required is that the workers will need to be prompt in the mornings. I will get the names and addresses from you later when we finalize everything."

Maggie grinned. "I'm pleased to know that," Maggie said, relieved.

Mrs. Beckham lifted an eyebrow as she looked at Maggie.

"Colin Doyle has requested to personally be your escort for the time being. How could we say no since he brought you to us?"

Maggie blushed. She didn't know if she was blushing because of Blanche Beckham's compliment, or the fact that Colin had requested to drive her to and from her work. "Thank you. I will be pleased to have Colin drive me."

"Good. That's settled. I do have one final surprise for you, but first I'd like Patrick and Connor to work here loading and unloading the supplies. They will also be needed to lift the large rolls of materials for the seamstresses."

"Patrick and Connor like their work at the pub, but I think they'll enjoy working here." She brushed her hair from her brow. "I am overwhelmed. A simple thank you does not seem adequate for what is in my heart."

"No, Maggie, I thank you. You've made me a better woman." She stood and Maggie followed suit. "Come. I want to show you your surprise before I show you the workrooms."

Blanche Beckham walked to a locked door located behind the main counter. She unlocked the door and headed up a flight of stairs. Maggie followed her. She opened a door at the top and it opened up to an enormous flat.

Maggie had never seen such a large, beautiful flat. She was amazed at the space. She walked through each area. There was a cooking room separated by a door, with another room for meals. The main room contained a large beautiful fireplace and a large floor to ceiling window, which overlooked the bustling city below. Off the main room was a small hallway leading to four doors. She discovered that the doors led to the bedrooms.

Mrs. Beckham stood back, observing her. "This is your new home, Maggie. For you, Patrick, and Connor. It's so much larger than the tiny flat you've been living in. There's room for the young men to each have their own rooms. And there will still be an extra room for any guests you may have. You'll never have to go outside in inclement weather to get to the shop. There is also an outside entrance to the flat for your visitors, and a back entrance for the workers." She touched Maggie's shoulder. "This is your new home, Maggie."

Maggie drew a deep breath, not believing what she was hearing. She'd never imagined living in such a glamorous place. All the furnishings were modern and brand new. The walls were papered with a design featuring beautiful flowers and vines. Long draperies covered the windows, and the hardwood floors shined brightly. But as beautiful as this home was, she'd miss her flat and her friends. "I've been very happy in my flat," she said quietly. "I have many friends in the building."

Blanche nodded. "I understand." She grabbed Maggie's hands and held them. "They will always be your friends, Maggie, no matter where you live, and they can visit you here. If they don't have transportation, Connor or Patrick can pick them up." She smiled again. "There is also a carriage house, with two carriages and horses for Patrick and Connor. We have employed a stable boy to care for the horses."

The good news didn't seem to end, and Maggie was having trouble taking it all in. Her heart was thumping wildly.

"Your friends will be happy for you. You deserve everything good this world has to offer." Mrs. Beckham gave Maggie's hands a friendly squeeze. "Sometimes change is hard, but you know that most times it is good. I hope you'll agree to live here."

Maggie thought about what Blanche had said. The woman's generosity knew no bounds, and she gave from the heart. As she met the woman's eyes she realized that Blanche received as much joy from giving as she did receiving. Maybe even more. Of course she was grateful. And yes, change was good.

"Of course I will," Maggie said, beaming. "So much happy news. I can't wait to tell Patrick and Connor."

****

Maggie stood back, watching as friends and neighbors filled the flat. The door was open, with many spilling out into the hallway to celebrate. The furniture had been pushed back, and several tables filled with food, sweets, and drink lined one wall. Music filled the air from the men as they played their fiddles, and others danced or tapped their toes and clapped their hands in time to the music.

Patrick joined her, a wide grin spreading over his face. "We truly are blessed, Maggie. We have food, music, and good friends. We'll never go hungry again. Da and Ma would be proud of what you've done for our family and so many others."

Maggie studied him. He'd grown into a handsome young man, as she'd expected that he would. He was happy and relaxed as he clapped his hands when the men finished a tune.

"We are blessed, Paddy, but I wouldn't have survived any of it without my brother by my side." She put her arm through his. "Watching the joy on our friends' faces is what makes me happiest."

He nodded. "Where's Colin? He should be here celebrating with us."

"He should, but he had an appointment. He's sorry to miss the party, but he's promised to stop by later."

"I'm going to grab my fiddle and join the men," Patrick said.

"Go ahead, Paddy." She smiled as she watched him walk away.

****

"This was good fun," Maggie said as she, Patrick, and Connor cleaned the flat later that night.

"It's too bad that Colin missed it," Connor said.

"He'll be by later. There'll be more parties." She patted Connor's back. "You and Erin O'Brien have been seeing each other for a long time now." She watched as his eyes clouded.

"We have much in common, and I am very fond of her."

"Do you love her?" Patrick asked bluntly.

Connor's face reddened. "I do."

"Then ask Charlie and Molly for her hand in marriage. Isn't that what you want?"

"It is," he admitted.

"Why are you waiting?" Patrick persisted.

Connor exhaled loudly. "The time's not right."

"You'll know when it is," Maggie quickly interjected. She knew that he wasn't at peace with himself because of his sisters. He was torn. He blamed himself for their fate. "What about you, Patrick?" she asked, taking the focus off Connor. "You visit the O'Briens almost every evening. Is playing the fiddle with Charlie the only reason?" she teased.

Connor grinned. "I think you're sweet on Rose. In fact, Erin tells me lately you and Rose have been spending a lot of time alone together."

Patrick shrugged sheepishly. "She's a nice girl." He set aside the broom he'd been sweeping the floor with. "I actually had a long discussion with Father O'Ryan."

Maggie's eyes narrowed. "Is something troubling you?"

He shook his head. "I was considering becoming a priest."

Connor snickered. "You do know you have to give up

169

girls."

Patrick made a face. "Father O'Ryan said to give it more thought."

"Did you?" Maggie asked.

"Aye. It's an impossible task."

Maggie and Connor laughed, and then Maggie grew serious. "Are you two happy about moving to the flat above the shop in a few days and working in the shop?"

Patrick frowned. "I'll miss the friends we have here."

"Since Erin will be working there, too, I'll get to see her even more than now with working at the pub." He smiled. "And with the carriages I can take her on rides." He looked at Patrick. "It is the same for you with Rose."

"It'll be good."

Maggie glanced around the flat. "We've done enough for tonight. The rest can wait until tomorrow."

Connor yawned. "I'm heading to bed, then."

"To have sweet dreams of Erin, I suppose," Patrick said with a wink.

"Would be very sweet if they are of Erin," he replied as he walked to the bedroom he shared with Patrick.

"Paddy, that tune you played tonight...the one you played with Charlie O'Brien. You've never played it before. It was one Da played when I was a wee lass. He played it rarely. How did you learn it? I don't remember Da teaching it to you since it's a hard tune to play."

Patrick shrugged. "Charlie started to play and asked me to join in. It came to me easily. It's been one of my favorites. Sometimes Da would play it for me when we were alone."

"You have a gift with the fiddle, Patrick...just like Da."

He grinned, pleased with her compliment. "I learned from the best." He stopped talking and nodded toward the door. "Who would be awake besides us at this hour? Hear that, Maggie?"

Maggie's listened to the sound of footsteps in the hallway, followed by muffled voices. "Must be one of the neighbors sweeping the floor," she said. "I'll have a look." She hurried to the door, followed by Patrick. She slowly opened the door and was surprised to see Colin on the other side.

"Colin, I'm sorry you missed the party," she said.

"I'm sorry, too." He smiled at her. "I had important business to attend to, and it went longer than expected. But I promised you I'd come by tonight."

"And you are a man of your word."

"I had some business with Mr. Beckham. Something has happened."

She could read nothing in his eyes. "Colin, is it bad news you bring?" she asked nervously.

"No!" he beamed. "It's the best news," he announced excitedly. "Time for even more celebration."

Relief flooded Maggie. "Don't just stand out in the hallway, Colin. Please, come inside and share your good news with us."

"Isn't Connor here?"

"He's gone off to bed," Patrick answered.

Colin's eyes brightened. "Wake him immediately! I have the most wonderful surprise for him. I must go fetch it, but I will return in a few minutes." He exited without saying another word.

Maggie looked quizzically at her brother. "Do you know about this, Paddy? Has Colin said something to you?"

"No, he said nothing to me. I'll wake Connor."

Maggie paced the floor while she waited for Colin to return. Patrick and Connor walked over to her.

"What's happened?" Connor asked.

A soft rap sounded on the door.

"We're about to find out."

****

Colin stood in the doorway, but then stepped aside. Two young women slowly entered the flat at his urging.

Connor's jaw dropped as he studied them. His arms instantly stretched out as he ran to them, enclosing them both in a tight embrace. "Bridgette! Katie!" he cried, as tears streamed down his cheeks.

Maggie was stunned. "Colin, how did you do this?" she whispered, leading him away from Connor and his sisters. She glanced back at Connor. "Now he can finally have peace."

Colin placed a light hand on Maggie's shoulder. "Some time ago I told Mr. Beckham about Connor's sisters. I hope you don't mind my interference."

"Of course not," she quickly replied. "What you did is good."

"Mr. Beckham has business connections in Liverpool. It took some time to locate them, and that is why I kept silent, in case they couldn't be found. His connections in Liverpool put a plan in motion to get the girls alone and then safely onto a ship. Mr. Beckham and I agreed not to speak of it until the girls were safely in America." He looked at them. "It has been a long time, and now they are young women."

"No matter how it happened, Colin, thank you for your part in it. A very important part, I must say. Come sit. I'll get some food after I properly greet Connor's sisters. It's a pleasure to meet you, Bridgette and Katie. I'm Maggie, and this is my brother Patrick."

Patrick stood awestruck at the sight. "It's a pleasure to meet you both," he said, extending his hand.

They shyly mumbled a greeting as they timidly looked at Patrick and Maggie.

"This is your home now," Maggie said. "Come sit at the table and let me get you some food and drink. You must be hungry after your long journey."

"Thank you, ma'am. We are very hungry," Bridgette replied.

Maggie smiled warmly at the pretty brown haired young woman. Katie had the same brown hair and pretty features. "Only one rule in this home. You must call me Maggie."

Bridgette smiled shyly at her. "Yes, ma'am...Maggie."

Katie nervously eyed Maggie. "You may not wish us in your home. We are not proper." She blinked back tears. "We lied to our neighbor when he saw us a long time ago. We didn't want you to be ashamed, Connor. We thought it best you forgot about us since we could never escape our fate." She broke down, sobbing.

Connor didn't relinquish his hold on them, and seemed to grip them even closer to him. "Not true, my sweet Katie. You and Bridgette had no say in what those evil men did. Every day I prayed that I would see you again...that we would be together again. I could never forget you or be ashamed of you. It is my fault for letting you go with that man."

"No, Connor," Katie sniffed. "You had no choice. He would have killed you before our eyes. He told us that."

Maggie hoped that what Katie had said would finally put to rest the blame Connor had placed on himself for his sisters' fates. They were here now. Safe and sound. He was complete. Now he could move on with his life. Now all of them could move forward to a bright future.

He looked at Maggie as the tears still streamed out of his eyes. "The Lord has blessed me by bringing Patrick and

Maggie Quinn to me. We are all family."

"Will the man find us here?" Bridgette asked fearfully.

"The man who took you tried to take me, too," Maggie said softly. "He's dead. He can't hurt you ever again. We will forget that horrible past." She doubted they would ever be able to forget it, but hoped that someday it could be pushed far back in their memories so they could enjoy a life filled with hope and promise. "You both are as honorable as anyone in this house. We are all equal here. What your brother says is true. We are all family. And Colin Doyle is a very special friend of ours, and is like family."

Colin lifted a surprised eyebrow, while Patrick grinned as he looked at his sister.

"Now you will sit and eat," Maggie insisted. She waited until Connor and his sisters had settled themselves at the table, and then placed platters of food in front of them. As she moved away from the table, she wiped a tear from her eye.

Patrick turned to Colin. "Colin, you've done so much good for our family. Is there anything we can do for you? Just name it."

"Your friendship is all I ask for," he said quietly as he kept his focus on Maggie.

Patrick smiled again as he looked at his sister.

"And that you'll always have," Maggie replied. "Now Colin, sit and eat. Then we will talk more."

"In a minute. Let them have this time alone," he said, nodding to the table where Connor sat between his sisters with his arms still around their shoulders while they ate.

CHAPTER SEVENTEEN

Maggie cheerfully prepared breakfast. She was excited about Christmas, which was fast approaching. There were so many things she needed to do to get the apartment ready. It was hard to believe that several months had passed since Colin had reunited Connor with his sisters and they had all settled into their new home above the shop. Bridgette and Katie still carried the demons of their past with them, but through the love and efforts of Maggie, Patrick, and especially their brother, they were relaxing more with each passing day. She couldn't imagine the horrors they'd suffered in Liverpool. They still had occasional nightmares in the still of the night. She'd tiptoe into their room and comfort them, assuring them that they were safe and sound. She'd hold them tightly until they drifted back to sleep.

Maggie had given them both work in the shop, and was pleasantly surprised at how quickly they adapted to their tasks. They'd rebuked the young men that came calling, but she knew the day would come when they would accept an invitation from a gentleman caller.

She intended to make this the best Christmas ever. She

glanced at Bridgette and Katie, who were busy setting the table. Connor and Patrick were huddled close together near the window talking in hushed tones. She assumed they were secretly discussing their Christmas surprises.

"Breakfast is ready," she called to them. They patted each other on the back as they walked to the table and seated themselves.

"I hope you two were discussing how big the Christmas tree should be."

"This will be the first time in many years we will have a Christmas tree," Bridgette exclaimed. Her eyes sparkled with excitement.

Katie nodded. "May we help to decorate it, Maggie?"

"Of course. It's a family tradition. I thought we might have a party and invite all our friends over on Christmas Eve before we go to church."

"That's a good idea," Patrick said. "Mrs. Beckham has asked Connor and me to find a small tree to put in the shop, too. We thought we'd go after breakfast if you can spare us."

"And we also want to do a little Christmas shopping," Connor added, "After we pick up the seamstresses."

Maggie laughed. "I think we can manage. The girls and I have some shopping to do this evening ourselves after we close the shop."

"Will it be a busy day today in the shop?" Patrick asked.

She lifted an eyebrow. "What day isn't? But I wouldn't change a thing."

Connor sat looking contentedly at everyone. "This really is going to be the best Christmas ever."

****

Maggie was showing the vast assortment of fabrics to a patron, while Bridgette and Katie were waiting on those picking up their gowns and dresses, when the bell on the door jangled. She looked in the direction of the door as a tall, thin, blonde haired woman entered.

"May I help you, ma'am?" Katie asked, walking over to her. "Are you here to pick up an order?"

The woman smiled. "Yes, thank you. You may help me." Her eyes swept over the racks of dresses and gowns, and then she walked to where the fabric samples were located. "I'd like to be measured for a gown. I'll need it by February."

"Yes, ma'am. If you'll be so kind as to come this way, I'll have your measurements taken. Then you can choose your fabric and what design you prefer, along with any special details, which I'll note on your order."

The woman sniffed indignantly. "I don't want just any seamstress to make it. I want Maggie Quinn. You are no one in the social circles these days unless you own at least one Maggie Quinn original gown."

"She's with someone at the moment. If you'd care to wait, she'll be free in a few minutes. Please have a seat."

"I'll wait," the woman replied.

Katie walked back to the counter as Bridgette finished writing a customer's order. She set the order slip in a bin located behind the counter. Bridgette swept the back of her hand across her brow after the woman she'd been waiting on exited the shop. "Whew! I don't know how Maggie keeps up."

"I hope that someday I can be half the woman she is," Katie said.

Bridgette grabbed her sister's hand and gave it a quick squeeze. "We are fortunate to know her. We are fortunate to all be family."

Katie looked toward the blonde haired woman sitting on

a couch impatiently tapping her foot.

Maggie appeared at the counter, moved behind it, and placed the order she'd just taken on top of the pile. "That took a little longer than I expected. She doesn't need the gown until spring, though."

"You have another waiting for you, Maggie," Katie said, nodding toward the direction of the blonde. "She asked only for you. I fear she's growing impatient."

Maggie smiled. "I saw her arrive. I'll take care of her. Thank you, Katie," she said, and moved to where the woman sat. "May I help you? I'm Maggie Quinn."

The woman rose, and as she did her eyes swept over Maggie. "You're nothing like I expected. I thought you'd be much older," she said haughtily. "Well, never mind. I just have to have one of your personally made gowns by February."

"I'll see what I can do. It is very short notice." Maggie was put off by the woman's arrogance, but maintained her pleasant business attitude. As she observed the woman's plain features, she realized that the woman's mouth seemed to be formed into a perpetual frown. "Why don't you start by telling me what you'd like, and then I'll show you some fabrics and I'll take your measurements."

The woman nodded.

Maggie took notes while the woman explained the design she had in mind. She took her time picking the fabric and other adornments. When she was finished, Maggie brought her to a changing room and measured her.

While Maggie was in the changing room with the woman, Patrick and Connor cheerfully entered the shop dragging a Christmas tree behind them. Katie and Bridgette rushed over to them.

"I was beginning to think you two were lost," Bridgette

said with a bright smile.

Patrick laughed. "Nah. We searched the city to find the perfect tree for our own home. We've already taken it upstairs. This is the one, just as good, that we picked for the shop. A little bigger, but nice. Where's Maggie?"

"With a customer in the changing room," Katie answered. "The last one of the day, I hope. It's almost closing time."

"I'll put the closed sign on the door," Connor said. "Have the seamstresses gone home? Colin said someone else would be driving them today since Patrick and I had to get the trees."

"You mean has Erin O'Brien gone, brother?" Katie teased. "No. She's waiting in the back for you."

He smiled as he put the closed sign on the door and then, whistling, walked to the back where the workrooms were located.

"Was it busy today?" Patrick asked.

"Very. Let's get a look at the tree. Now we have two trees to decorate," Bridgette said gleefully as she clapped her hands.

Maggie and the woman exited the changing room and walked to the counter.

"I need the gown by the first of February. Not one day later," the woman said stiffly. She handed Maggie some money. "Is this enough for the deposit?"

Maggie counted the money. "It's fine. The dress will be ready. You'll need to come in for a final fitting to make certain everything is the way you like and it fits properly. Now, if you'll give me your name."

"Sarah O'Malley."

Maggie's heart froze and her hand trembled slightly. "Did you say O'Malley?"

The woman's eyes narrowed. "Yes. Is something wrong?

You've gone pale."

Maggie cleared her throat. "No. It's just that I haven't heard that name in a long time. I knew someone with the name long ago." She smiled weakly. "Now, if you'll sign the order."

Maggie watched as Sarah O'Malley signed her name. Her eyes were instantly drawn to the ring the woman wore. She stared at the ring and didn't realize that her eyes had been glued to it until Sarah spoke.

"It's beautiful, isn't it? I get many compliments on it. My husband Ian gave it to me. It was the only thing he managed to escape Ireland with. It belonged to his late mother."

"Yes. It is a beautiful ring," Maggie said quietly.

"Well, I'll be off. Merry Christmas."

"Merry Christmas," Maggie said, and watched as Sarah O'Malley left the shop. She clutched the counter as hot heavy tears stung her eyes.

"Maggie, come see the tree Connor and I picked out," Patrick called.

Maggie quickly composed herself. She couldn't let anything dampen their spirits or ruin Christmas. For now, she'd keep it to herself. Maggie examined the tree. "It's beautiful! We'll start on decorating it tomorrow."

The girls clapped their hands. "It'll be so much fun. And we can sing while we do," Katie said.

She smiled at them. "Where's Connor?"

"Taking Erin home." Patrick looked closely at her. "Are you unwell, Maggie? You've lost your color."

"If you're not feeling well, Maggie, we can go shopping another day."

Maggie drew a deep breath and smiled. She didn't want the girls to be burdened with her troubles. They'd been through too much already, and she didn't want anything to disrupt their newfound happiness or their first Christmas together. This Christmas was special to all of them. They were all together. She'd never seen Connor so happy. His life had come full circle now that his sisters were safely home with him. She wanted to keep them all close for as long as she could. She knew it wouldn't be long until Connor asked Erin O'Brien to be his wife. She loved Erin, and couldn't have picked a more perfect wife for him. But when he married, he'd of course have his own home with his wife.

Seeing Ma's ring today had unnerved her, and she knew she couldn't keep it from Patrick. Nor should she. He had a right to know. "You and Katie go upstairs and put on your heavy coats," she said cheerfully. "I'll be up in a minute. I need to talk to Patrick. Then we'll go."

"Come along, Katie. Let's see the big Christmas tree Patrick and Connor have brought home." The girls excitedly hurried up the stairs to the apartment.

Maggie turned to her brother. "I need to tell you something."

"I knew it," he said, watching her closely. "What's happened, Maggie? Are you ill?" he asked with a look of alarm.

She saw the fear in his eyes and heard it in his voice. "No, I'm not ill, Paddy. It's nothing like that." She swallowed hard. "That woman who was just here…did you notice her?"

"I did. Did she say something to offend you?"

"No." She swept a hand through her hair. "It's her name."

"Her name?" he asked through narrowed eyes. "Why should her name disturb you?"

"Her name is Sarah O'Malley."

Relief flooded his face. "Is that all? Maggie, don't let the ghosts of the past come back to haunt you. O'Malley is a common Irish name. You know that. There are probably many with the name in the city." He patted her shoulder. "You've been working too hard. Maybe you should put off shopping with the girls. They will understand," he said sympathetically. "Let's go upstairs and I'll fix you a cup of tea. It'll settle your nerves."

"No, Paddy, you don't understand. She *is* Ian's wife," she insisted.

He raised an eyebrow. "How do you know? Has she said she is married to Ian?"

She nodded. "She claims her husband came from Ireland," she choked out, then broke into sobs. "She wore a ring she said her husband Ian brought with him. He told her it was his mother's ring, Paddy. It was Ma's ring. That woman was wearing Ma's ring. How can he be so cruel?"

"Are you certain it was Ma's ring?"

She saw his body begin to twitch with anger. "Yes, you know that ring was like no other."

His body stiffened and his eyes burned. He balled his hands into tight fists. "I'll kill him," he shouted.

Connor and Colin had just come through the worker's door when they heard Patrick's shout. They ran to Maggie and Patrick.

"Maggie, what's happened?" Colin asked. Maggie was crying too hard to respond. He put a protective arm around her. "Please tell me why you are crying." He turned to Patrick. "Patrick, what has her so upset? We heard you shouting when we came in."

Patrick's face was still red with rage. "Ian O'Malley. He's the cause."

Connor stiffened. "He was here in the shop?"

182

"No. His wife was." He looked at Connor. "She was wearing our ma's ring."

Connor put a hand on Maggie's arm. "I'm sorry, Maggie."

Colin released Maggie. "I'll be back." He headed for the door.

"Colin!" Where are you going?" Maggie called after him.

"I'll be back later," he said over his shoulder. "Go shopping with Bridgette and Katie."

Maggie was worried. She had her suspicions of where he was going. Maggie didn't want any harm to come to him. She'd never forgive herself if it did.

Chapter Eighteen

"It's snowing!" Bridgette exclaimed as she, Maggie, and Katie hurried into a small café holding tightly to their gaily wrapped packages.

Maggie smiled at the young women's rosy cheeks and bright eyes. She enjoyed their company, and found herself looking forward to their shopping trips and talks. They truly were family.

They found a table and sat. They ordered coffee and heaping plates of stew and biscuits.

"I wonder what the men are fixing for supper," Katie said with a giggle.

"Whatever it is, I'm sure we'll have a mess to clean up," Bridgette said with a smile.

"I think they'll go around the corner to the inn for their supper." Maggie lifted her eyebrows. "Can you imagine either of them doing the cooking?"

"No," Connor's sisters said, and then laughed.

"I enjoy working in the shop with you, Maggie," Katie said.

"Me, too," Bridgette quickly added. "I never knew anyone

could make such beautiful dresses and gowns."

"Thank you both. I couldn't think of anyone I'd rather have working with me." She smiled at them. "Here comes our food."

Their food was placed before them and they chatted while they ate. Maggie observed them as they talked about the gifts they'd gotten for Patrick and Connor. They still wanted to shop for the O'Brien family. They'd become close to Erin and Rose, and the four of them shared their work breaks together. Maggie was pleased, since the O'Briens were still and always would be her closest friends.

Maggie had a special Christmas gift for Bridgette and Katie. She'd secretly been sewing each of them a new gown and dress. Yes, this would be a wonderful Christmas. Maggie wouldn't let anything get in the way of Bridgette and Katie's happiness. But she still couldn't put Colin out of her mind. She hoped he wasn't trying to track Ian down. Ian wasn't the man she'd once thought he was. He'd changed. She didn't know what he was capable of, and she was worried about what he might do to Colin. Maggie would never forgive herself if anything happened to him. It suddenly dawned on her how important he had become in her life. They all still attended Saint Matthew's Church on Sunday, and Colin joined them afterward for dinner, as he still did a couple of times during the week. No, she couldn't imagine him not being a part of her life.

They finished eating and accepted fresh cups of coffee. Maggie smiled across the table at them. "You've both gone quiet." Bridgette looked at Katie. Their expressions looked pained. "Okay, girls, what's wrong? I saw the look that passed between you."

Bridgette flushed. "It's not our business, Maggie, but

we're concerned."

"About what?" she asked softly. "We have no secrets in our family."

Katie fiddled with her coffee cup. "We know you were upset earlier. Someone has hurt you." Her eyes misted. "When you hurt, we hurt, Maggie."

"No secrets, remember?" Bridgette reminded her.

Maggie chewed her bottom lip. The girls were right. She had just said no secrets, but she was keeping one. "I'll tell you what's had me upset," she said.

****

Maggie sat at the table with Patrick and Connor. They sipped hot cups of tea as they waited for Colin to return.

"The girls had a good time shopping with you, Maggie," Connor said. "They're so excited about Christmas." He sighed. "I never thought I'd be having any more Christmases with them."

"And you'll be having many, many more...all of us will, together," she said. "I hope I didn't dampen their spirits, but they held me to my claim of no secrets in our family." She drew a deep breath. "I'm sorry I had to tell them, Connor."

He thought about it for a minute. "No, it's good that you did. They love you, Maggie. They were shocked to learn that a man who once asked you to be his wife could be so cruel to you. When I went to bid them goodnight, they were sobbing because they can't bear you being in such pain."

"They have such tender, beautiful hearts." He exhaled loudly and shook his head. "I wish I could undo all that's been done to them, and all of us."

Patrick's lips tightened. "I wish that woman had never come into the shop today."

"No, Paddy, it is good that she did. I know Ma's ring

hasn't been sold." She grew pensive. "I do wonder how he made his fortune. Mostly why he did not sell Ma's ring."

Patrick shrugged. "Maybe Colin will have the answer."

Maggie nervously twisted her fingers. "I'm worried about him. Ian is a cruel man. We know that now. He's not the man I thought I knew." She bit her bottom lip. "I'll never forgive myself if anything happens to Colin."

"Colin will be fine," Patrick assured her. "If I know him, he's likely gone to enlist Mr. Beckham's help. If Sarah O'Malley belongs to the social circles, Mrs. Beckham is certain to know her. All our questions, I'm sure, will be answered when Colin returns."

"It's so late," Maggie said. "Do you think he'll return tonight? If he has no news, possibly he's decided to wait until morning so as not to disturb us."

Patrick stretched. "I don't know. You're almost asleep on your feet, Maggie. Go to bed. Connor and I will wait up in case he does return tonight." He patted her hand. "I promise to wake you if he comes."

"Thank you, but I wouldn't be able to rest. I'll wait up for a while longer. If he doesn't show up soon, then I'll go to bed."

They finished their tea and then moved to the parlor, where they sat quietly, each consumed by their own thoughts. Maggie's eyes grew heavy and several times she dozed off. She stretched and rubbed her eyes, and glanced at the couches. Patrick and Connor were sleeping soundly. She sat back and dozed off again. The next time she opened her eyes two more hours had passed.

She rose and walked over to Patrick, gently shaking his shoulder and then Connor's. "You two get off to bed. He's not coming."

The words were barely out of her mouth when a soft tapping sounded on the door. She looked at Patrick and Connor and then rushed over to it, flinging it open. "Colin! Come inside."

Colin stepped into the room shaking snow off his coat. Maggie took his coat and hat and hung them on the rack by the door. "You look frozen, Colin. Come warm yourself by the fire while I get you a hot cup of tea."

He removed his gloves and blew on his hands. "Thank you, Maggie. That would be good." He smiled warmly at her.

"Do you have any good news for us?" Patrick asked.

Connor stood in front of the fireplace staring at the blazing logs while rubbing his hands together. He turned.

"Sit," Maggie ordered, bringing a steaming cup of tea and placing it on a table next to a large ornate chair.

Colin sat and instantly picked up the cup of tea. He held the cup in his large hands, obviously enjoying the warmth on his frozen fingers. Colin seemed oblivious to the three sets of eyes peering at him. He brought the cup to his lips and peered over the top at them. He took a swallow and set the cup down. "You will be getting your ring back, Maggie."

"I don't understand. You don't have it with you?" It didn't make sense to her. If he'd retrieved it, why had he not brought it to her?

"No. I didn't meet with Sarah O'Malley."

"You met with Ian, then?" Patrick asked.

He shook his head. "I talked to Mr. And Mrs. Beckham about the situation. As expected, they were very disturbed, as they both are very fond of all of you." He paused. "After I told them you'd seen your ring on Sarah O'Malley's finger, they instructed me to wait."

"Wait for what?" Connor asked.

"To wait for their return. They decided to pay a social call on the O'Malleys. I spent the evening waiting, as you have, for news. When they returned they said to let you know that your ring would be returned."

"Did they talk to Ian?" Maggie asked.

"No." He ran a hand over his chin. "He wasn't present, but his wife was. As expected, she was deeply upset by his deception."

Maggie sighed. "Even though she's not the friendliest woman I ever met, I almost feel sorry for her. She must have been sick at heart when Mrs. Beckham told her about the ring."

Colin lifted an eyebrow. "Don't feel too sorry for her. She insists it's not the same ring."

"She believes I'm being untruthful? I certainly know Ma's ring. And she did claim Ian brought it back from Ireland. It was Ma's ring that Paddy gave Ian to sell."

"Don't be upset, Maggie. He's her husband, and she likely is having a difficult time believing he would lie to her."

She nodded. "I suppose in her place I would feel the same." She frowned. "You said my ring will be returned. How, if she denies it's mine?"

He grinned. "She told the Beckhams to settle the matter, she is coming to the shop with Ian in the morning to confront you, Maggie."

"What if Ian refuses?" Patrick asked.

"That will prove his guilt," Connor said.

"Connor's right. Either way, Ian can't get out of his lie. He never should have given the ring to his wife."

"He could still say I'm lying about the ring," Maggie said.

"I don't think he will," Patrick stated. "She will learn about what he did to you."

189

Maggie nodded. "That's true."

"He never expected to get caught," Patrick said angrily. "He expected Maggie would never get to America, and he knew I wouldn't leave Ireland without her." He was quiet for a minute, and then a wide smile suddenly broke over his face.

Maggie stared at him. "Have you lost your senses, Paddy?"

"No," he chuckled. "I would just like to see his face when he learns we are here, alive and well. I want to see his face when she asks about the ring."

Connor grinned. "I wouldn't want to be him. I'm sure uncertain times are ahead for him."

"How did Ian O'Malley become so wealthy in such a short time?" Patrick asked.

Colin shifted his weight. "He didn't make his own wealth. Sarah Worth comes from old money. Mrs. Beckham and Sarah were in the same social circles. Sarah's father was anxious to marry her off, but Sarah never seemed to be able to keep a suitor interested for long. If what Mrs. Beckham says is true, Sarah isn't always a very pleasant person to be around." He paused and sipped at his tea. "Sarah's father was very angry when Ian began charming her, explaining to her that Ian O'Malley wasn't in their social class and would ruin their reputations. He'd been hired to work in the stables, so Sarah wasn't in contact with him. It wasn't until the driver took ill and Ian took over as driver that he met Sarah. It wasn't long until she fell for his charms. In the end Mr. Worth accepted him when Sarah threatened to run off with him."

"Since I know what deception Ian is capable of, it is easy to see why he charmed her. I fear it was for her money, not love. He has turned into a greedy, evil man," Patrick said distastefully.

"Paddy, you shouldn't say such things. He may truly love her," Maggie said.

Colin shook his head. "No, Maggie, Patrick is right. Mrs. Beckham thought the marriage odd, but it wasn't her business. To her, it was plain to see that Sarah wasn't happy. Some of the women in her social circles shunned her, and Mr. Beckham claims Ian O'Malley spends his time gambling."

"He is not the man his family raised. They would be ashamed." Maggie frowned. "I am grateful that he did not sell Ma's ring, and I pray that soon it will be back with me. Morning can't come soon enough."

"It already is morning," Patrick said, rising and stretching. "I'll be in the shop with you, Maggie."

"Mr. Beckham has asked me to be in the shop, also," Colin said.

"Me, too," Connor said.

Maggie smiled. "Thank you all."

"Well, I'll be off to bed for a few hours' sleep," Patrick said.

"Goodnight, Paddy." Maggie rose and gave him a hug.

"I'm off, too," Connor said, kissing Maggie's cheek.

"Goodnight," Colin said. "I'll be here when the shop opens."

Patrick and Connor said their goodnights and left the room.

Maggie turned to Colin. "Would you like another cup of tea?"

"No. Thank you." He rose. "I'd better be on my way and let you get off to bed. Hopefully your dreams will be sweet tonight." He looked at the tree.

"I hope you'll join us to decorate it," she said softly.

He smiled. "I'd like that." He took his coat and hat from

the coat rack and put them on. "I'll be back first thing in the morning."

"Thank you for everything, Colin."

"Good night, Maggie. Sweet dreams." He put his hand on the doorknob.

She reached out and touched his arm. "Colin?"

He turned and faced her. "Yes, Maggie?"

She smiled softly. "A long time ago you asked me a question. If you ask it again, my answer will be yes."

****

Maggie anxiously looked toward the door each time the bell jangled. Bridgette and Katie were busy taking orders from the customers. Patrick and Connor stood near the back of the shop, and Colin stood behind the counter. All of them were on edge, not knowing what to expect.

Maggie dreaded seeing Ian, wondering if she'd be able to hold her tongue. She ached to lash out at him for what he'd done to her. Maggie wasn't sure she could keep her emotions under control. But she had to remember that life was good for her and Paddy now. And their family had increased with the addition of Connor, Bridgette, and Katie. She had to put the past to rest, and once Ma's ring was safely back in her possession, she would. Maggie vowed never to take the ring off her finger.

She glanced at Colin, and he smiled affectionately at her. Her heart was full, and the love they felt for one another was evident in their eyes. Tonight they would have a very special dinner and announce their engagement to the family.

An hour later Maggie walked over to Colin. "They're not coming. I suppose Ma's ring is lost to me forever."

He laid a hand on her arm. "It's early. Maybe they got a late start," he answered reassuringly.

Maggie sighed. "It's possible. Soon morning will turn to afternoon. Katie will be putting the sign up for the break. Maybe they will come this afternoon." She watched as Bridgette finished up with a customer. She picked up the orders on the counter and looked them over.

After Bridgette's customer left, Katie was walking to the door to change the sign when the door suddenly opened. Sarah O'Malley closed the door, and without looking either way walked straight ahead to the counter.

Maggie looked up and watched Sarah's stiff movements. She was surprised that Ian wasn't with her. Sarah didn't say anything at first, and Maggie waited for her to speak. She noted that Colin, Patrick, and Connor had moved closer to the counter, but stayed far enough away to give Sarah some privacy.

Sarah set the ring on the counter. "This doesn't belong to me," she said without emotion. "I'm sure you know the details." She smiled weakly. "I'm sorry, but I won't be needing the gown. I'll be leaving the country for a few months. I'll pick something up in Paris."

"I'm sorry, too, Mrs. O'Malley." She meant it. She was sorry that Sarah had been hurt by the man she obviously loved, and now because of his unsavory deeds had to suffer the embarrassment.

Maggie sorted through the orders and pulled Sarah's out of the stack. She opened a drawer, counted out the deposit money, and handed it to her.

Sarah took the money, nodded, and with her head held high walked to the exit and left.

Maggie held the ring close to her heart for a few seconds, and then slipped it on her finger.

Writing is Susan's number one passion. When she isn't writing, she enjoys reading, spending time in her garden, and visiting family and friends. She has many novels, short stories, and magazine articles to her credit. Raised in western New York, she now resides in New Jersey. For information about Susan's current and upcoming titles, please visit http://www.susandroney.com or http://susandroney.blogspot.com